His primary go

He raced past the ~~park entry. Entering the~~
campground circle, he immediately zeroed in on
the too-familiar Tahoe. It wasn't so much parked as
abandoned.

Among the clusters of people, Garrett didn't
immediately see Cadence. She wouldn't have gone
in pursuit on her own, would she? He wouldn't
believe that. She could be reckless, but—

He was suddenly able to breathe. There she was,
crouched with an arm around an older woman.
Garrett had seen compassion on Cadence's face
before, but he was surprised anyway. As fit as she
was, she'd just loaded herself up with medical
supplies and hiked almost to Wagonwheel Lake, an
elevation gain of at least three thousand feet.

Cadence's head turned just then, and her dark eyes
locked onto his.

Whether he liked it or not, his heart gave a hard
squeeze.

WILDERNESS HOSTAGE

JANICE KAY JOHNSON

Harlequin

INTRIGUE

In memory of my parents, who were ardent mountain climbers. They spent the early years of their marriage in Olympic National Park, where Dad served as a ranger often involved in mountain rescue. I loved picturing those early photos.

Harlequin®
INTRIGUE™

Recycling programs for this product may not exist in your area.

ISBN-13: 978-1-335-45725-7

Wilderness Hostage

Copyright © 2025 by Janice Kay Johnson

Harlequin Enterprises ULC
22 Adelaide St. West, 41st Floor
Toronto, Ontario M5H 4E3, Canada
www.Harlequin.com

Printed in Lithuania

MIX
Paper | Supporting responsible forestry
FSC® C021394

An author of more than ninety books for children and adults with more than seventy-five for Harlequin, **Janice Kay Johnson** writes about love and family and pens books of gripping romantic suspense. A *USA TODAY* bestselling author and an eight-time finalist for the Romance Writers of America RITA® Award, she won a RITA® Award in 2008. A former librarian, Janice raised two daughters in a small town north of Seattle, Washington.

Books by Janice Kay Johnson

Harlequin Intrigue

Visit the Author Profile page at Harlequin.com.

CAST OF CHARACTERS

Cadence Jones—A national park law enforcement ranger, Cadence is terrified when an ugly crime puts her in the bull's-eye just as she becomes certain she's pregnant. Ironic that the father of her baby is in charge of the manhunt that threatens the woman he'd been sure he couldn't love.

Garrett Wycoff—Cadence has cut him off...but he'll do anything to save her from a brutal pair who robbed a gun shop and killed a cop. Seeing them on a collision course with Cadence, he grapples with the terror of really losing her.

Cole Souza—The more vicious partner in the arms heist, Cole crashes through roadblocks to evade the cops, who seem to be everywhere, but the flight ends at a dead end in a national park. They must disappear on foot into the vast wilderness.

Evan Hensen—A terrified boy snatched as a hostage, and an insurance policy, by brutal men. He has no hope—until a beautiful ranger sacrifices herself for him.

Mason Fitch—Less volatile than his partner, Mason will still do what he must to escape the trap lying ahead.

Chapter One

Trouble could erupt with little warning. If she weren't so aware of that truth, Cadence Jones could in theory have let herself relax into a day that, so far, had been remarkably trouble free.

An EMT and law enforcement ranger in the wild and mountainous Olympic National Park on the western edge of Washington state, she'd made it through most of the morning without a single alert on her radio. She hadn't so much as issued a ticket for speeding or to campers for lacking the required permit. Plus, once she'd turned off the busy Highway 101 a few minutes ago, she was traveling on a narrow gravel road that plunged into the filtered green light inside some of the most magnificent temperate rainforest in the world as well as offering regular glimpses of the swift-flowing Queets River.

She always remained conscious that she didn't dare let herself be lulled into complacency just because this was part of one of her regular patrol routes. This week, she'd been assigned to the west side of the park. She'd already driven slowly through the parking lots for several of the spectacular Pacific Ocean beaches that drew tourists like flies. This being midweek, even Ruby Beach, with magnificent stacks and rock formations, hadn't been quite as crowded as it would be in another few days. There'd only been a few cars parked in lots for one of the other beaches. That would change in the next weeks once schools were out for the summer.

The current peace didn't mean she wouldn't get a call about a drunk driver, a domestic dispute, an attempted suicide, a stolen car or any other crime, most of which were as common in the national parks as they were in major cities. Staying alert was her *job*.

Truthfully, it was the knot of dread in her stomach that kept her fingers flexing on the steering wheel. She should have already called Garrett. Procrastination never helped, but the talk she had to have with him felt big. No matter how she tried to convince herself that she'd be fine whatever he decided, the pressure squeezing her chest and balling greasily in her stomach didn't relent. She had tomorrow off—barring a major callout for a search and rescue, say—but couldn't remember his schedule. Maybe he could take time to meet her for lunch—it might be just as well if he couldn't afford time for more than a quick meal.

Between one blink and the next, she saw his face, lean, handsome, with blue eyes that too often looked remote. That expression alone had been fair warning that it would be a mistake to get involved with him. She should have known herself better than to think she could enjoy a relationship that was never meant to be lasting.

Cadence took a quick swallow from her water bottle. A deer with two spotted fawns appeared on the road ahead, tugging Cadence's attention back to the here and now, where it belonged. How could she not smile? With their incredibly fragile legs, the fawns bounded after their mother and disappeared into the dense, vividly green undergrowth.

The campground at the end of the Queets Road, her current destination, one of the most remote in the park, was small and primitive, hardly worth checking out, but Cadence liked to keep an eye on trailheads, too. Car prowling was less common than it once had been, given how many vehicles had alarms, but people too often left tempting items lying in plain sight instead of at least tucking them away in the trunk. At the campground, she'd wander to check out who was here and whether everyone had permits and was following regulations and spend some time answering questions.

Knowing the landscape as well as she did, she slowed further at a section of road that occasionally washed out. No problem right now.

An alert sounded on her radio, sending a prickle of electricity through her. Dispatch, seeking *her*.

She acknowledged receipt and gave her current location.

"That's good news," a dispatcher she knew well said, urgency in her voice. "A child is missing at the Queets campground. The parents assumed at first that she wandered away, and other campers are helping look for her, but the mother started getting uneasy about a man who walked by their campsite several times and once started a conversation with the girl when the parents were distracted. The kid is five years old," she added. "The father looked for the man, but can't find him. Every campsite is occupied, and a couple of other people also noticed the guy wandering. They say he wasn't a camper and didn't look as if he'd come back from a hike, either."

Cadence thought immediately about the car that had just passed, but there'd been at least two passengers as well as the driver in it, and her snap impression had been that they *were* hikers or climbers heading out of the park. They'd had that scruffy, several days past a shave look.

Still, she felt enough uneasiness to describe the car and suggest that if a state trooper or county deputy was near enough to stop it once it emerged onto 101, they do so.

At that moment, she saw another vehicle bearing down on her at a speed that far exceeded safety on a narrow gravel road with potholes and often nonexistent shoulders. What's more, the driver had to have spotted her vehicle by now and identified it as law enforcement, but he wasn't slowing down as she'd expect.

Damn it. None of her options were ideal, but she couldn't help making a mental leap to the man who had been too interested in a young girl who had since disappeared. She *couldn't* let this vehicle pass, or depend on county or state law enforcement waiting out at the highway. They were all spread too thin over vast territory.

Gritting her teeth, she made her choice and braked sharply even as she wrenched the steering wheel to steer into position to form a roadblock. She flipped on lights and siren to accentuate her point.

For an ugly moment, she thought the oncoming car might slam right into her SUV. There wasn't room for it to brush by her, or she was sure it would have. It rocked as the driver slammed on brakes and slid to a stop, inches from her passenger door.

The driver, the only apparent occupant of the vehicle, fixed a blistering stare on her. She went on the radio quickly, described the situation and the make, model and color of the car before requesting backup. No license plate number; she couldn't see it from her current angle.

It would be pure luck if a county deputy was close enough to reach her before the situation was resolved, but she could hope.

She used her microphone to order the driver to exit his

vehicle. "Now," she commanded sharply. "Keep your hands where I can see them!"

He didn't move. Cadence opened her door and slid around it so that most of her body was protected by the engine block of her SUV. Then she drew her weapon and aimed it at him.

He was still glaring when, a full minute or two later, he finally opened his car door and stepped out. His head and upper body started to bend, and she suspected he was leaning forward as if to reach for something on the seat or the floorboards.

"Hands in the air!" she yelled. "Back away from your vehicle, sir. I need you to lie on the ground, face down. Do it now!"

There was a noticeable hesitation. Her mind worked furiously. Even if he complied, then what? He was a big enough man that she didn't dare get within reach, which meant she couldn't cuff him. If he didn't offer his wallet, she wouldn't be able to reach for it.

"Write me a ticket," he growled, as he took a step backward, leaving his driver's side door open. "Yeah, I was speeding, but there wasn't any traffic to worry about."

"There is abundant wildlife." His sneer didn't improve her mood. "And *I* happened to be on the road," she added.

"Let me get my registration. My wallet is in my back pocket."

"Lie down on the road. This is not optional."

"You've got no right to treat me like this. What are you, some kind of pseudo cop?"

"I'm a federal law enforcement officer, with all the authority held by an FBI or DEA agent. There is nothing pseudo about my uniform or my authority. *Now lie down*." She waggled the gun.

She hardly dared blink as he slowly lowered himself to his knees.

"Shut the door," she told him.

"Shut it yourself," he snapped with a few ugly words thrown in.

Dispatch informed her that a Jefferson County deputy had turned onto Queets Road and was approaching with all possible speed. She responded, "Copy."

What if it was Garrett? She'd count herself lucky, that's what.

Did she dare approach close enough to kick that door shut? Cadence reluctantly decided not.

"Down," she repeated.

He got as far as his hands and knees, let his head hang for a second, mumbled under his breath, then lunged suddenly toward whatever he wanted to get his hands on so badly.

Cadence fired a single shot underneath the car door, aiming to skim the surface of the road. He fell back, screaming at her. No blood.

"Do as I say!" she snapped. "That was your last warning. Down on your face! Hands in plain sight!"

He complied at last, hate in his eyes. If he held a weapon, she'd be dead, she thought. She evaluated him, guessing him to be in his forties with the muscles of someone who worked out on a regular basis. A tattoo showed above the collar of his white T-shirt. He wore cargo pants and boots meant for kicking butt, not climbing or hiking.

What if it turned out speeding was the total of his offenses? Would she be in trouble for firing her gun? Her gut said she'd done what she had to—and that they'd find he had a handgun stashed beneath the seat of his car.

Out of nowhere, nausea struck her, as it had erratically

the past week or ten days. With unpredictable bouts of misery and an occasional knees-down visits to toilets, this had to be a flu bug. She wouldn't let herself believe anything else.

She was sweating now, even in the relative cool in the shade of the giant trees, and her hands trembled. She kept her elbows locked and resolutely swallowed the bile that wanted to rise. *Not now,* she told herself desperately.

If only she could move on him, cuff him, look inside the car and especially open the trunk of his car, but the risk was too great. Especially now that backup would be arriving within the next five or ten minutes.

Those minutes crawled. Her nausea slowly receded. She prayed no innocent camper would appear. Onlookers were prone to getting out of their vehicles, asking questions, distracting an arresting officer, even ignoring orders to stay back. Instinct told her this situation was genuinely dangerous, no misunderstanding. A few birds called, making her realize they'd been silent initially during the confrontation, but life was resuming around her. There was another sound, too. She cocked her head. Thin and high. Her certainty hardened.

A few minutes later, she heard an approaching engine. *Let it be the deputy.*

The crunch of gravel and a single blast of a siren were incredibly welcome. A green-clad deputy appeared beside her. Not Garrett, but she'd worked before with Gary Vickers.

"Thanks for coming." She sounded steadier than she felt. "The suspect keeps trying for something on the floorboard of his car. I'd appreciate it if you could cuff him."

"My pleasure." Maybe in his late forties, Vickers was solidly built and had always appeared sharp and competent when he'd backed her up—or, once, when she'd backed him up.

The man's hate-filled stare never left her face even as the deputy walked around the back of her park service issued SUV and approached the prone man from his blind side. With her having already demonstrated her willingness to fire her gun, there was no fight when Vickers cuffed him and ordered him to stand. Within minutes, the suspect had been searched and shoved to the sheriff's department vehicle.

Turning to watch as he was locked in the cage, Cadence let her arms sag before she holstered her gun. That she'd fired it meant a whole new level of paperwork, but right now she didn't care.

She hustled to the open door of the car, joined by Vickers, whose eyebrows rose as he saw what she did—a semi-automatic pistol lying almost under the driver's seat. Then Cadence yanked a thin latex glove from her pocket, donned it and said, "You're my witness," as she pulled the lever to unlatch the trunk lid.

They both heard the whimpers even before Cadence made it far enough to see the little girl curled around a spare tire.

GARRETT WYCOFF HAD stiffened when he heard the request for backup. Jefferson County stretched across the Olympic National Park, which meant deputies policed a stretch of the county on the ocean side, but most operations were east of the park instead, including Hood Canal and other waterways. The two parts of the county were severed by the park, the drive from one side to the other lengthy. Right now, he wasn't where he wanted to be.

He'd just responded to the report of a theft in the tiny

community of Brinnon along Highway 101, which almost circled the peninsula. A resident had returned from a long weekend visiting family to find a window broken and a new smart TV stolen. Nothing else was obviously missing from the log A-frame, which made Garrett suspect the burglar was an acquaintance and very possibly a local resident who knew about the new flat-screen TV.

After taking the report, he'd been about to turn onto the highway to resume patrolling when he heard the request for backup from a park ranger and the subsequent communications. He'd never heard such stress in Cadence's voice, and his whole body had tightened with a need to be where he could help. Vickers was good, though, which was a relief. That didn't mean Garrett could make himself do a damn thing but listen and wait. A child had gone missing, but he didn't know how that connected to a speeding driver on Queets Road who wasn't complying with orders.

He reassured himself that Cadence was sharp, fit and experienced. As a slender woman who didn't even top five foot five inches, she had a vulnerability he didn't. And yeah, that scared him, an admission he didn't want to make. He'd been enjoying their casual relationship. He didn't think he'd ever had better sex in his life, and their jobs gave them a lot in common. They both loved getting away into the backcountry. They'd climbed a couple of peaks together. Conversation never flagged when he was with her, but because of their conflicting schedules days went by between them meeting up even for a meal. He frowned. He hadn't seen her in nearly a week, which he'd been unhappy about.

Yet another acknowledgment to make him edgy. He wasn't even sure he was capable of seriously falling for a woman, but never intended to let that happen. He'd drawn a line at the beginning, which she had respected. He couldn't, wouldn't, let that line blur.

No, he'd be tense when something like this was happening that involved any of his coworkers or the park rangers he'd gotten to know.

Vickers spoke briefly on the radio to report the suspect was in the back of his vehicle ready for transport to the jail in Port Hadlock. Long drive knowing someone is drilling the back of your head with a death stare.

Moments later, he identified himself again and said that the suspect had had a semiautomatic beneath his driver's seat and had apparently been going for it when LE Ranger Jones had fired her weapon to force him to return to his prone position. The deputy sounded exultant when he added that the missing child had been in the trunk of the suspect's car. She was terrified but appeared uninjured.

Cadence came on to say that she was transporting the girl to the Queets campground to reunite her with the parents, and that she'd escort them to the hospital in Forks for the child to be evaluated. A special agent chimed in that he was on the way to the scene to examine the car and would also arrange a tow.

Garrett let out a long breath and bumped his head on his steering wheel a couple of times. All was well. Nothing for him to get worked up about, and no excuse for him to have wasted the past twenty minutes. He'd call Cadence tonight and congratulate her for recovering the girl who'd been snatched and arresting the kidnapper. Maybe she'd be free in the next couple of days.

He'd barely merged onto the highway when he saw that the car in front of him was weaving subtly. License plate… he looked it up and was unsurprised by the confirmation that he'd had more contact with the driver than he'd like.

Lyle Kellam was drunk more than he was sober. Alcoholics Anonymous always did temporary wonders for the man—until he relapsed. He'd looked good the last time Garrett had seen him at the grocery store in Quilcene, up the road a ways. Given that this was midafternoon, you'd have thought he could hold out for his first drink of the day until he made it home, but apparently temptation had overcome him.

Garrett used lights and siren to get Lyle's attention, and then rode his bumper when that didn't initially work. Once Lyle pulled over, his right front tire turned halfway into a ditch, Garrett walked up, tapped on the window and bent over to see a man who always made him think of an elf with oversize ears, a tuft of white hair and eyes as blue as his own.

Lyle rolled down the window and peered owlishly at him. "You again? I'm almost home."

It's true that he was. Lyle hadn't actually crossed the double yellow line. He gritted his teeth and made a decision.

"I'll follow you home," he said, "but you know what the consequences will be the next time we verify that you're driving under the influence." Significant jail time was what he meant.

Lyle slumped. "I know. I'll call my sponsor. I swear I will."

Maybe. But Garrett didn't renege on his decision to let this slide. He did follow closely as Lyle drove the half a mile to the turnoff to his ramshackle house. Then Garrett blinked his headlights and accelerated to highway speed.

The next hour was uneventful enough to have him wondering if his grandfather really needed him anymore. Seattle PD would take him back, he knew. His goal had always been to work as a detective, not to spend a career pulling over speeders or investigating the theft of a single item from a home. He hadn't minded while his grandfather had depended on him, but that didn't mean he had ever intended to move to this rural county permanently. Yeah, there were rewards, like really getting to know residents, but—

His phone rang and when he saw Cadence's name, Garrett pulled onto the shoulder of the road and answered.

"Hey," she said.

"Exciting day."

"You could say so." The smile he had no trouble seeing sounded in her voice. "Scary, too. Still, you should have seen the expression on her parents' faces."

"Yeah. That makes the job worth it."

"It does." There was a pause. "I'm off tomorrow. Can we meet for lunch?"

Her tone had changed, but he couldn't put his finger on how. "I'm not," he said, "but sure, if you can make it over my way."

"Blue Moose?"

"Perfect." The café in historic Port Townsend, once a logging town and the customs stop for any ship entering the Puget Sound, was a favorite of his and Cadence's. Food was good, there were plenty of vegetarian choices for her, and the quaint atmosphere included smoothly polished wooden booths.

They set a time and she ended the call abruptly, leaving him…wondering. Telling himself he'd imagined there was anything odd in her tone.

Chapter Two

Cadence was the first to arrive, sliding into one of the smooth wood booths so that she faced the entry. Garrett would try to persuade her to switch, since like most cops, he preferred not to have his back to the entrance or other diners. It had become a lighthearted competition between them, whoever got there first winning, although in truth she didn't care that much.

On a pang, she thought maybe today she'd surprise him by voluntarily giving way, since the chances were good this would be their last meal together.

When he walked in a couple of minutes later, effortlessly dominating the space with his broad-shouldered, six-foot-three frame along with sheer magnetism, only one other booth was occupied. He'd needed to take his break early. Cadence had been glad. She wanted to get this over with.

His gaze locked onto hers, giving the impression that he saw only her. Maybe that was true; in the initial split seconds, he'd undoubtedly already evaluated the quaint restaurant and the few customers and staff, all of whom she knew were watching him. He'd grab attention no matter what, but today he was in uniform besides, wearing a vest that added bulk and the belt that held his holstered gun and a bunch of other paraphernalia. *She* certainly couldn't look away.

As always, the sight of him made her instantly breathless, a little dizzy. When he reached the table, he stood gazing down at her for a minute. A few lines she didn't recognize creased his forehead.

"I listened to your stop yesterday," he said. "I hear you had to discharge your weapon."

She made a face. "I did. After that, I was left thinking about the uproar if I'd risked shooting a guy who hadn't done anything worse than drive recklessly."

"But you knew better," he said, as if he'd never doubted her. His calm and faith in her let her breathe again, although her smile was probably more a grimace.

He slid into the open side of the booth without comment on their silly competition. A waitress hustled up, offering menus neither needed. Both ordered. Once they were alone, he reached across the table for her hand.

"You okay?"

"Of course I am."

He nodded acceptance.

"How's your grandfather?" She always asked, even though she hadn't met the man, had never been invited to the hundred-year-old house where Cliff Wycoff had lived for his entire lifetime. The house where his grandson now lived, too. She'd been so tempted to drive by just to see it, but always resisted.

That house and knowing how important his grandfather was to Garrett were a big part of why Cadence had made the decision to talk to him now. Garrett had never invited her home or to meet the man who he had described as his only family. Their sexual encounters took place elsewhere, including her substandard trailer on occasions when her two roommates were working, tents when she and Garrett backpacked and climbed, even motel rooms a few times.

How sleazy was that? Better question: how had she convinced herself she didn't mind?

"Better enough to be getting ornery." Garrett half smiled. "Doesn't like me telling him he's doing too much." She knew his grandfather had had a heart attack followed by a four-way bypass.

"I imagine that's normal."

"It's a good sign," he admitted.

Subject closed.

Their food arrived, and she discovered she was ravenous. Breakfast had been half a toasted bagel, dry, to quell the queasiness that vanished an hour later. The swing between nausea and sharp hunger had characterized this week. Perhaps it was mild food poisoning. Right? Nothing else… In any case, it was not pleasant.

They talked in a desultory way about politics in the sheriff's department, a couple of concerning crimes that had happened in neighboring counties and the expected flood of visitors in the upcoming week or two when summer season really took off.

Finally, he asked, "This the only day you're free?"

"I'm not entirely free." She pretended to concentrate on the last bite of her giant cookie. "Dan Becker—do you know him?—is leaving us. Not the usual time of year, but he's wanted to work at Denali and they had a sudden opening. We're throwing him a party."

She could invite him, but he rarely accepted when she suggested this kind of event, even though many of her co-workers had seen them together. She'd been foolish enough to convince herself that he didn't love the heavy drinking that often ensued, or the fact that he was an outsider. Another waving red flag, she thought; God forbid he appear too much like an actual boyfriend who wanted to get to know her friends. Even if he didn't enjoy himself, it wasn't as if they couldn't have made a brief appearance and then left.

Disappointment showed on his face, but he didn't say, *Maybe I could get there*, even though he knew Dan. Nope, he was disappointed because he wouldn't get laid tonight.

Too bad, so sad.

Except, she loved the passion they shared, the extraordinary sense of intimacy she'd never felt before. The tenderness that flavored the lust.

He shifted on his seat and produced his wallet. "Let me get this one. I'd probably better get back to work."

"There's something I wanted to ask you about first," she made herself say, "but why don't we walk out together?"

His vivid blue eyes narrowed slightly, but he only nodded, tossed a few bills on the table and gestured her to go ahead.

Cadence waited until he'd walked her to her car, an aging Toyota Corolla. Her chest felt tighter and tighter. Oh, this was hard. *I could wait and see instead of pushing*, the coward in her thought. Maybe she was expecting too much, too fast. But then she pictured him saying one day, *Hey, I'm sorry but I've met someone else*. They'd been dating— okay, sleeping together—for four months now. If he hadn't started falling in love with her in that length of time, it wasn't happening.

Get it over with.

She unlocked, opened her car door to facilitate a quicker getaway and folded her arms on top of the door. "You made it plain when we started seeing each other that you weren't interested in any commitment. That long-term wasn't for you."

He recoiled, even taking a step back.

Cadence tried not to flinch. Instead, she lifted her chin. "I'm asking now if you've changed your mind. If there's any chance—"

"You're not happy with how things are?" he asked roughly.

"No. I'm sorry to put you on the spot like this, but the truth is, I never should have agreed to this. I'm…not really into casual. I've started feeling too much. If I keep seeing you, I'll get hurt." *More than I already am.* "We're good together, Garrett. Really good. I wanted to be up-front with you, see if you feel the same."

Was that panic in his eyes? She couldn't tell, but whatever it was didn't bode well for her.

"I don't want to lose you, but I can't go there," he said. His hands had fisted at his sides.

Pain roared through her, but she held on to her dignity and nodded. "That's what I thought you'd say. In that case, I need to call it quits." She shrugged. "I'm sure we'll run into each other as long as we're both working here. Let's not make it a big deal, okay?" She threw in a "Thanks for lunch" without looking at him again. Instead, she lowered herself into her car, pulled her door shut and shoved the key in the ignition. From her peripheral vision, she saw him backing up but not turning away. In fact, when she turned onto the street, he still stood in the middle of the small parking lot, watching her go.

Which meant she had to zigzag several blocks before she could pull to the curb, set the emergency brake and let herself give way to grief.

It was a good half an hour before she pulled herself together enough to know what she had to do next. If she was wrong about the flu bug, if she were pregnant, she had to face reality. It would change her life in ways she hadn't

yet let herself detail, but she had time to come to terms
with all that.

And yes, if that was true, she'd tell Garrett. She owed
him that much, and he'd owe her some support, too. But
now she knew: however much obligation he felt toward her
and his unborn child, he didn't love her, couldn't love her.
She'd needed to know in case he'd reacted to the news of
a pregnancy with a sense of obligation that led him to say
things he didn't mean.

She was getting ahead of herself. She'd been trying really
hard to convince herself that she was feeling cramps, her pe-
riod would start any minute, she really had a virus responsible for the icky stomach.

But she knew. She knew.

WHAT IN HELL had just happened? Garrett had the surreal
feeling that a car had just hit him and his body was flying
through the air. That he'd slam to the ground any minute.

Instead he stood stock-still in that damned parking lot
even after Cadence's car was gone.

How had this blown up? She was right; things *were* really
good between them. Making love with her wasn't like anything else he'd ever experienced. When they weren't getting
together, he thought about her. He made excuses to call just
to hear her voice. Something had happened to him the minute he saw her the first time. It wasn't just her looks, although
she was beautiful and in a distinctive way. Slender and fine
boned, she had skin that was tinted gold, deep brown eyes
that tilted up slightly at the outer edges and thick dark hair—
not black, but close—that flowed almost to her waist when
she released it from the usual braid or knot at her nape that
kept it out of her way. He had wanted to put his hands on her

more than he'd wanted much of anything in his life, which was something.

He groaned and let his head fall forward, reaching up to knead taut muscles in his neck. He'd let himself get lulled into complacency, damn it. He knew better. Even his grandfather had been asking about "that woman" he'd been seeing, and when Garrett was planning to bring her home to meet him. He'd avoided saying, *Never*, partly because integrating her more into his life would have been natural even if he couldn't see marriage on the horizon.

Was she insulted because he *hadn't* introduced her to the man who was his sole family?

Of course she was.

Honestly, until a few years back, he'd never had family, so that hadn't been an option. He'd disliked bringing women home to his apartment. Instinct had always insisted he compartmentalize. There was the job, there was sex and then there was his stark, lonely home life—although he'd never identified it to himself as lonely.

After his childhood, lonely was a synonym for peaceful.

Things had been different since he tracked down the grandfather he hadn't known he had, and particularly since he'd willingly quit his job with Seattle PD to come to this barely populated county on the edge of the world because he was needed by someone. First time in his life. Maybe that's what had softened him, let him start feeling too much for Cadence Jones. More than was safe.

He'd already known that was a problem, just…hadn't dealt with it.

Well, she'd taken care of that, hadn't she? She'd asked an honest question, and he'd answered honestly: he wasn't ready for anything like what she was suggesting.

Garrett realized how conspicuous he must be, standing here like an old-growth tree in the park that had been blasted by lightning but refused to fall. He retreated to his department SUV, fired up the engine but sat unmoving behind the wheel.

Had something in particular happened to make Cadence confront him like this? She'd met someone else? Had an opportunity to transfer to another park, as her coworker had? Maybe yesterday she'd been hit by the knowledge of how quickly a scene like that could turn sideways. Truly seeing her mortality might have made her reevaluate a relationship that wasn't going anywhere.

Or she could have been saying, *I'm falling in love with you*.

If he'd asked her, would she have answered? And did it matter, anyway?

Garrett had always known that he was protecting himself, but he didn't know any other way and couldn't see baring his belly for some woman to savage him.

Would Cadence do that?

He shook his head hard. Didn't matter. Except he knew that the next time he heard her on the radio when she was making a frightening stop, or rappelling off one of the rock faces of an Olympic Mountain crag on her own to try to save a climber who wouldn't survive until other help arrived, he'd hate it every bit as much as he had yesterday.

CADENCE GROCERY SHOPPED, made a separate trip to a pharmacy for a pregnancy test, but after seeing a couple of people she knew at QFC, decided instead to pick up a uniform she'd had dry-cleaned and, once she got home and found both roommates there. So she bundled up her dirty clothes and sheets for a trip to the laundromat. Better to stay busy. She could slip away this evening to be alone. Bethany and

Tierra loved parties and were likely to hook up with guys and not make it back to their own beds tonight at all.

She wouldn't stay any longer than she had to tonight, and she could surreptitiously pour out any drinks she was handed. Booze of any kind didn't sound good at the moment anyway.

She browsed news on her phone while she waited to move her laundry to the dryer and then spotted a couple of several month-old magazines that she could at least pretend interest in until the two dryers stopped. Lugging the baskets of folded clean clothes and sheets out to the car, she was grateful to have completed a chore she too often put off. Honestly, the hours she worked, she rarely managed a real day off. It was a miracle she hadn't been called to join a rescue.

Midweek, she reminded herself. Just wait until this weekend, and then July and August when the park really got slammed with visitors. This and all other national parks were always understaffed, which was a real problem when life-and-death crises arose so often. Glacier melt–swollen rivers, serious climbing rock, powerful ocean waves with an undertow and inadequately prepared tourists kept her too busy to sleep or eat sometimes, far less think about the heaps of dirty laundry at the foot of her bed.

Could she *do* the job if—?

Too soon to worry about.

She changed into a cute sundress and went to the party whether she was in the mood or not. She smiled for all she was worth, while surrounded by boisterous coworkers— rangers and concession workers both. The concession workers especially were a hard-drinking bunch—their pay was lousy, many were college students who liked the idea of a summer job in a spectacularly beautiful piece of this country—and because Dan Becker was an ardent mountain climber, a bunch of climbers who somehow never quite held jobs showed up, too.

Cadence gave Dan a big hug, admitted that Denali was not on her wish list—too much snow and ice, too many times rangers had to fly in small planes and helicopters—and unobtrusively separated herself from the cluster around her before slipping away into the darkness, finding her car and retreating to her not-so-cozy home away from home.

Sad to say, given that she was in her thirties, the word *home* still brought to mind a 1940s bungalow where she'd grown up, where her parents and Oliver still lived in Idaho. Certainly not this cramped, shared space where she slept and not much else. But as much as she loved her family, she didn't really want to go home.

She wanted her own. Seeing Garrett in her mind's eye and knowing she wanted that home with him, a knife blade of pain plunged into her chest.

She'd get over him. She would.

Cadence carefully hung her sundress back up in the minuscule closet and put on the pajama shorts and T-shirt she wore to bed. Then she locked herself in the bathroom even though no one else was here, read the instructions on the box and followed them. The short wait after she peed on the stick was excruciating.

The answer…not really a surprise. But it was as terrifying, as life altering, as she'd known it would be.

Chapter Three

A pair of cop killers, on the run.

Utilizing lights and siren, Garrett drove too fast for narrow roads, set on reaching Highway 104 to block the SUV speeding away from the crime scene from being able to cross on the Hood Canal Bridge. Grimly determined to prevent them from escaping, he swore under his breath every time he had to swerve around a slow-moving vehicle driven by someone who managed to be oblivious to the lights and siren.

This week, Garrett was filling in for an absent sergeant in the patrol division. Technically, he'd been hired as a patrol deputy, but because of his background, he was used for a variety of other roles, including filling in for or backing up the two detectives and the detective sergeant. He expected to be out on the road today, too; there were never enough bodies to cover multiple shifts and the miles of Jefferson County as well as the waterways. Plus, while the largest city in the county, Port Townsend, had its own police department, after hours and on weekends Dispatch diverted those calls to the sheriff's department, too.

Unfortunately, early morning was the worst time of day to have a crisis. Night shift, already scanty, would be heading for the station to sign off; day shift might not be there yet.

He'd gotten into the station at the crack of dawn. He hadn't been sleeping anyway, so why not? He needed distraction from the hamster wheel of thoughts about the woman who'd dumped him. He'd just sat down to look at the night's activity when the phone rang. He recognized the number right away. He'd gotten to know the Clallam County chief criminal deputy, and felt sure a call this early in the morning wasn't meant to exchange chit-chat.

"Wycoff," he answered.

"We have a problem that's heading your way," he was told tersely. "There was a break-in at a gun shop between Port Angeles and Sequim. An explosive was used to blast a hole in a cinder block wall."

Garrett absorbed that. "What if ammunition had been stored on the other side of that wall?"

"The fact that it wasn't is one reason I assume they'd cased the shop. We'll be examining security footage." The chief deputy continued, "The alarm went off. What's more, the owner of the tattoo parlor that's attached to the gun store was sleeping there. He ran out to see what was happening and got shot. A deputy who happened to be close by responded to the alarm and was gunned down, too." Anger simmered in the brief pause. "Didn't even have a chance to get out of his vehicle or draw his weapon. He's dead. The tattoo shop owner is badly injured, but he was able to tell us that while he lay on the ground bleeding, he saw two men throwing guns and boxes of ammunition into the back of a big black SUV. Tahoe, is his best guess. They took off maybe ten minutes ago, speeding east on 101."

Unless the men were locals, what had they been thinking? The only real highway was pinched between the mountains and the water—the Pacific Ocean to the west, the Strait of Juan de Fuca to the north and Hood Canal to the east. Did they realize the problem with their escape route, or had they assumed they could load the guns and be on their way, anonymous?

Shaking his head, he said, "I'll see to setting up road-blocks. We can't let them get to anyplace more populous."

"I was hoping you'd say that."

"License plate?"

"No outside security camera. Washington state plate, the witness thinks."

The chief deputy promised to keep him updated as they searched the scene.

Garrett spoke to Dispatch to reposition deputies already out on patrol, then made calls to get more out of bed. He assumed Clallam County deputies were on alert in case the pair changed their mind and thought they could do a U-turn and head west instead, to join the tourists traveling through Forks and down the Pacific Coast.

He called the sheriff, who agreed with his intentions, then leaped into his own vehicle to be part of the blockade where Highway 104 turned east from 101. This would be a dangerous stop, if it could be made at all; the two men were apparently in possession of a virtually unlimited number of weapons and all the ammunition they wanted. They'd killed a cop, which meant they had nothing else to lose.

Even as his attention stayed on the road ahead, he listened to radio traffic and calculated tactics. He tensed when national park law enforcement was brought in, but thought it unlikely they'd have reason to get involved in this mess. Even the air force base on Whidbey Island received a notification. The base provided a helicopter when one was needed for either the Olympic or Cascade National Park. They agreed to have one ready to go when needed.

One deputy after another checked in, unfamiliar tension

in voices. Garrett wasn't quite in position when one of his deputies came on.

"Black SUV just blew past me. It went by the turn to 104 and is continuing south on 101. I repeat: it's continuing south, and I am in pursuit, although by the time I got up to speed, I lost a visual."

"Did you get a license plate?"

"No, sorry."

Garrett ordered urgently, "Pursuit only, do not attempt on your own to pull over this vehicle." He looked at his dashboard clock. Damn. More time had passed than he liked. As the day advanced at high season, Highway 101 on the scenic Olympic Peninsula could rival stretches of I-5 in Seattle with rush hour approaching. Climbers and hikers wanted to get an early start. Unfortunately, 101 was mostly two-lane, which made a vehicle exceeding the speed limit beyond dangerous. A high-speed chase was too risky. Anyone who'd seen the result of a head-on, high-impact collision never forgot it.

"Have you regained a visual?" he asked a minute later.

"No. Traffic is picking up."

He made a decision he didn't like, but the only one he could make. "Discontinue pursuit." Several deputies were already south of the sighting, and he instructed them to set up where they could see the highway and wait. There were a few turnoffs, but not many; one led back north to Highway 104, and he placed one deputy in a place to watch for just that as he accelerated again on a back road that would connect with the highway at the town of Quilcene.

Since for now the sheriff seemed to be leaving the logistics in his hands, Garrett asked that he contact neighboring jurisdictions, just in case. He was sure he'd heard about a couple of hits on gun shops in surrounding areas. He always made a mental note about crimes that stood out. One had been in Bremerton in Kitsap County, if he remembered right, and another down toward Olympia, the state capitol. Shelton, maybe? He didn't think either had resulted in deaths, but a break-in this bold didn't have the feel of a first attempt to him. A number of previous successes would explain this hit, both brazen and poorly thought out. Apparently, it hadn't occurred to the men that there'd be a glitch that would mean trouble escaping.

Word filtered in from deputies. There were no sightings of a vehicle that matched the description given, certainly not one speeding. There weren't any real alternatives to the highway, not with how close the water was on one side and wilderness areas to the other. That didn't mean the men, running scared, hadn't taken a minor road or even a dirt one with the intention of hunkering down long enough to make law enforcement relax the intensity of the hunt. Several small towns hugged the highway and isolated homes could be vulnerable right now.

Primitive logging or forest service roads offered access to wilderness and national forest areas outside the park, too. Those tended to wind around like a pile of yarn dumped on a floor, but blocked by the national park and the formidable mountains to the west, those roads didn't *go* anywhere. Sooner or later, the hunted men would be dumped back out on Highway 101. The number one priority for sheriff's department deputies was to watch for that reappearance.

He stayed on the radio, adjusting deputies and praying nobody else committed a crime this morning. If so, the victim wouldn't get a prompt response—unless the caller reported a home invasion by two big guys waving guns.

Quilcene was the largest of the few tiny towns that hugged Dabob Bay, a long finger of water separate from Hood Canal.

Highway 101 took a sharp bend here that required traffic to slow down, but the town was also the radius of a number of residential streets and, south of Quilcene, Penny Creek Road, which narrowed to one lane that eventually turned to gravel and split several times without any directional signs. Like every other road heading west into the wilderness, all were dead end.

Where the hell had those men gone, and what would panic drive them to do?

SHOCKED BY THE unfolding manhunt that was dominating radio traffic, Cadence was almost surprised when an alert regarding an injured hiker cut through the intense, strained orders and responses. She was sent to North Shore Road on the southern boundary of the park. Within the park, the road split and became narrow and jarring to drive as she followed the north fork of the Quinault River until she reached the necessary trailhead. Families who wanted a short hike could go only as far as Irely Lake, but the trail continued, eventually connecting with others deep in the interior of the park. It provided access for climbers to a number of peaks, too.

In the back of her vehicle, she always carried an advanced life support bag as well as miscellaneous other medical supplies, a folding gurney on wheels and a more typical backpack that she'd have to carry on a rescue deeper in the park. This hiker, however, had twisted or broken an ankle before the party had reached the lake, not a long walk by her standards.

Assuming, of course, that the information was correct. Too often, what really had happened was garbled by the time it reached her, if it hadn't been in the original telling. She parked, glanced at the cluster of empty vehicles from a Volkswagen Bug to a camper, got out and decided to take only the most necessary medical supplies. She could jog back to get the gurney if necessary.

Her radio crackled. Dispatch directed all deputies to maintain position. Despite an even tone, the voice carried unusual tension. She should be out there, too, but had to wait for orders.

The men who'd committed a gun shop break-in, killed a Clallam County deputy and injured another store owner had vanished somewhere between the turnoff to Highway 104 and Leland, a mere dot on the map where a deputy waited tucked almost out of sight off the highway.

Kitsap County deputies hovered on the far side of the Hood Canal Bridge in case the fugitives succeeded in breaking that way. Clallam County deputies, especially angry after the murder of one of their own, were spread to the north. Mason County, to the south, was on alert. State patrol troopers put themselves under the direction of the Jefferson County Sheriff's Department.

Early on, Cadence had heard Garrett's voice, calm and decisive. Unless someone else had taken over, *he* was directing this manhunt. Somehow, that didn't surprise her; he exuded an air of command. Plus, she also knew that he filled in for sick or vacationing people in the department. Heaven knows, she thought, not quite facetiously, maybe he'd become sheriff for the day.

She felt sure that he wasn't issuing those orders from the safety of the department headquarters in Port Hadlock. No, if there was any conceivable way he could achieve it, he'd be in on the takedown.

She wanted to be able to dismiss her fear for him, which was completely unfounded at the moment. What were the odds he'd be the one in position to see the fugitives when they reappeared? Even if he happened to be, he was capable. Having seen him in action, she knew that. Coming from a major urban police force, he was likely the best trained member of this rural sheriff's department.

But telling herself to knock it off didn't accomplish a thing. She was scared and couldn't wipe from her mind a picture of him reeling from a blast of automatic gunfire. The shock, the loss of his powerful personality until only vacancy was left.

She couldn't seem to find her usual confident, centered self. It had to be an aftereffect of her close call last week. Where normally she put a tense encounter behind her, she kept reliving this one. Things could so easily have gone wrong. She knew all too well that it took only a split second. If kidnapper Raymond Miller had ducked and grabbed the gun initially and come up firing, or later completed his lunge for the weapon beneath his car seat despite her warning shot, she could be dead. Unlike him, she'd been wearing a vest, but she couldn't return fire without lifting her head above the hood of her vehicle. He could have—

Damn, damn, damn.

He hadn't. Even if he had gotten his hands on that gun, she excelled at her job. She trained regularly at a range, something he was unlikely to do. He was a pedophile—who she'd interrupted from being able to hurt that little girl— not a sharpshooter. And the incident wasn't the first time in her career she'd been threatened. It wouldn't be the last, either—unless this pregnancy derailed that career.

And, yes, for all her self-denial, last week she'd strongly suspected she was pregnant. The awareness made her feel more vulnerable than usual. She wanted this baby with a ferocity she hardly recognized in herself.

Caught up in her thoughts, she stumbled over a half-buried rock. As she recovered her footing, she lectured herself. How about paying attention to her surroundings, a concept that was usually second nature to her?

At a shout from ahead, Cadence saw four people approaching, two men and two women. One man and the taller of the two women were supporting the other guy, who was managing to walk while putting little-to-no weight on his right leg.

For once, the information she'd received was correct, except the hikers had decided to start making their own way down to the trailhead and their vehicle. All four looked to be in their early twenties, one couple wearing hiking boots, the other two only athletic shoes. Naturally, the injured guy lacked the boots that would have better supported his ankle.

Approaching, she smiled, pushed back her anxiety and introduced herself. She helped as they gently lowered the man to a seat on a fallen log, after which she crouched, pushed up the leg of his trousers and eased down his sock. There was definitely significant swelling and the beginnings of discoloration.

She gently probed, had him rotate his foot and decided to crack open an ice pack.

Placing the ice, she said, "I don't think your ankle is broken, but I can't be sure. You need to get an X-ray. I suspect a strain, which can be almost as slow to heal as a break."

Noticeably sweating, he grimaced.

"You expected back at a job soon?"

"Next week, but I work on a computer and mostly remotely."

"Ah." Cadence raised her gaze to the others. "Have you given him any painkillers?"

"Tylenol," said the woman staying close to his side.

"Okay. Well, once the ice does its part, I'll help you get

him the rest of the way down the trail. Then I recommend you drive him to a clinic or hospital. Unfortunately, you're going to have to go a distance."

The whole time, Cadence listened with half an ear to the occasional terse comments on the radio. Nothing new.

Eventually, she wrapped the ankle with an ACE bandage to give it additional support and took the place of the obviously exhausted girlfriend to help the injured man hobble the rest of the way. He was placed in the back seat of a Subaru Forester, his ankle elevated on his girlfriend's lap. Cadence collected enough information from them for her required report, gave them directions to the nearest medical clinic, and as she watched them drive away, radioed in so Dispatch knew she was once again available.

Why wasn't she being sent as reinforcement in the ongoing search for the cop killers? But she knew the answer. This was a busy week in the park, and there'd be plenty of calls on her time. *Someone* had to be available to look for straying children, provide medical services to folks who overextended themselves and more. Plus, there were few park entrances south of Quilcene, and since the washout at the Dosewallips River, no entrances could be driven up to until the Staircase Ranger Station. It could be reached by a couple of roads leading to Lake Cushman, which lay outside the national park and thus was surrounded by rustic resorts, vacation rentals, boat launches and campgrounds.

Getting trapped on a dead-end road in one of the wilderness areas or the national park would mean the two men on the run would have to abandon their vehicle and most of the stolen weaponry. Why would they do that? No, since they'd already missed their chance to cross Hood Canal, their goal had to be continuing south toward Shelton, a good-size town, and beyond that the city of Olympia—whatever they had to do to elude the net being cast by law enforcement.

Garrett was clearly intent on *not* letting them escape. In fact, of bottling them up in a rural area where hiding for any length of time would be difficult.

Cadence had to believe the men would be spotted anytime. What worried her most was how a stop would be made. Could even a couple of deputies working together persuade desperate, heavily armed men to pull to the side of the road and docilely submit to an arrest?

Chapter Four

The day was incredibly frustrating. In the next few hours, there were a couple of possible sightings that didn't pan out. Nerves stayed on edge. At length, the sheriff took over as incident commander while Garrett set out to hunt down background on the two men—assuming his instincts concerning them were good.

He spoke again to the deputy chief in Clallam County, who reported that it appeared the burglars had tried to disable the alarm before they set off the dynamite. They might have believed they had succeeded, which meant the blaring alarm had thrown them. Their decision to go ahead with the burglary despite the alarm said a lot about them. If they'd ever looked at a map, they had to have known fleeing was tricky, given the lack of alternative routes. Too, they'd responded to witnesses with instant, deadly violence, no apparent hesitation.

Garrett pursued his memories of previous, similar crimes by making multiple phone calls.

"If it's the same guys," a Bremerton detective told him, "they've made some changes. The gun shop that was hit here is only technically in the city limits. It's actually pretty isolated, which allowed it to have an outdoor range as well as an indoor one."

"This one was outside town, too—and the city of Sequim is pretty stretched out along the highway. The only other business close was the tattoo parlor that shares the building."

"Your injured man."

"Yeah."

He grunted. "We got them on security camera, for what good that did us. They drove a Hummer with a blade mounted on the front. Smashed right through the wall. I learned later that a National Guard armory was broken into that way, too. Years ago, but you have to wonder if that's not how they got the idea. Anyway, they did disable the alarm, but we could still watch them on the security feed. Not much help, as you can imagine. They wore something dark over their heads, gloves so they left no prints. The blade on the Hummer hid any license plate, and once they'd loaded as much as they could get in, they backed away just far enough to keep us from seeing the back plate. Once they swung around and took off, the picture just wasn't good enough for us to make out that kind of detail on the plate, even though the techs really worked at it. All I can tell you for sure is that two men did the job. Both were big and noticeably bulked up. We made some calls to gyms in the area, but nothing panned out."

"That fits the description of these two we have from the neighboring shop owner who survived being shot."

"I can have someone send you our footage, for what that's worth."

Garrett thanked him, and said, "The shop owner is out of surgery and the prognosis is good."

"That's something," the detective said, "but the cold-blooded murder of a deputy?"

What was there to say about that?

"Not so surprising they're driving something different," Detective Jacobsen continued. "You kinda look when a Hummer passes. You know?"

Garrett knew.

"I remember hearing about a gun shop robbery in the Shelton area maybe a year and a half ago, but there's been another similar heist since that caught my eye because of our open case. I want to say down Hoquiam way. Aberdeen, maybe?"

"If we drew a circle to encompass these hits," Garrett said, envisioning a map, "what do you want to bet the perpetrators live somewhere in the middle?"

"Wouldn't bet against you," Jacobsen said. "As it happens, Shelton was first, if I remember right. Makes me wonder if they aren't locals there. If so, it would have made sense for them to go farther afield the next time they decided to restock their merchandise."

Garrett's sense of humor was at a low edge for a lot of reasons, but he grunted a laugh. How *were* these guys selling the weapons? Online? What if they owned a gun shop themselves?

Still sounding steamed, a Mason County detective spoke freely about the armed robbery that had happened in his jurisdiction. An armed robbery was what it had been, only there'd been three participants, one of them a woman. They'd rushed in at closing, heavily armed, yelling orders, spraying a few bullets when an employee behind the counter reached for his weapon. He'd been wounded but survived; the woman had held a semiautomatic on him and the remaining man in the shop—a customer—while the two big guys grabbed and loaded. Then all three backed out and they fled at high speed.

"They were in a black SUV. We got a license plate, but

it turned out to have been taken from a stolen vehicle that never was located. Neither were they. They had to have known the area well, maybe had a bolt-hole close by. Use a remote to raise your garage door, close it behind you and you've disappeared. Man, I'd like to get my hands on them."

Garrett ended that conversation by saying, "I'll keep you informed," although they both knew that even if he arrested these two slugs, tying them to the other robberies would be possible only if one of the cooperating law enforcement agencies succeeded in tracking down where they stored the stolen weapons and found some with serial numbers from guns taken in the Shelton or Bremerton heists.

Or with a confession, but that seemed unlikely in the extreme.

It was an hour before he got a call back from Hoquiam, in Grays Harbor down the Pacific Coast, where events had transpired much as they had in Bremerton. No woman, and from what little they could see on a poor security camera recording, one of the two men was big and muscular, the other noticeably leaner. Vehicle? A pickup truck.

Wonderful. Garrett still had no doubt that these crimes were all linked, but now had to consider the possibility that there was a ring of crooks, not just a pair. Impatient with himself, he had to ask what difference it made. If they got their hands on the two men who'd killed a cop while stealing one hell of a lot of weapons, they'd be able to trace where they lived and anyone else who was involved. One reason to do their damnedest to make sure at least one of the two survived.

Garrett took a deep breath and rolled his shoulders before he let his head fall back. He was sitting in his department vehicle at this point, positioned south of Quilcene. He'd moved several times as the day went on, waiting.

Just as too many of the law enforcement officers on the Olympic Peninsula were doing. His muscles were starting to cramp up. He got out now and again to walk a few feet and stretch, but that wasn't enough.

Unfortunately, with radio traffic still sporadic even if it remained tense, he had had too much time to brood about Cadence.

Last night he'd gotten into it with his grandfather, resenting what felt like judgment. Or maybe it was that Granddad had said a few things that struck closer to home than Garrett wanted to admit.

He'd been closemouthed about Cadence, but his grandfather had been well aware he was seeing a woman. There were those nights he hadn't come home. And yes, he'd answered a few questions: she was a law enforcement ranger in the national park and she enjoyed hiking and climbing, as Garrett did.

"Something happen?" his grandfather had asked while they ate.

He had managed to shrug. "Just wore down, I guess." He'd pushed the bowl of green beans across the table.

Instead of reaching for them, his grandfather had studied him with shrewd blue eyes. "You seemed happy while you were seeing her."

"The relationship was never meant to be anything long-lasting." He'd heard the edge in his own voice.

"Huh." Granddad slowly dished up a few green beans—he wasn't fond of most vegetables Garrett pushed on him—and took a bite. Garrett had almost relaxed when his grandfather spoke again. "Doesn't seem like your bad mood is letting up. You sure you didn't make a mistake?"

Garrett growled something inarticulate that shut Granddad up, but that didn't mean he wasn't still thinking, his eyes seeing more than Garrett liked. That was a serious downside to actually letting yourself care about someone, open up to him.

Grimacing now, Garrett told himself his problem where Cadence was concerned was that *he* hadn't lost interest. He would have eventually; he always did, but she was right when she said they had a good thing going. They did.

Make that past tense.

She wasn't the only woman he'd been involved with who wanted more from him. He'd just thought Cadence was different. She certainly hadn't shown signs of nesting in the shabby trailer that was her current home. She was a federal law enforcement officer who shrugged off the daily risks, same as he did. She'd talked about other national parks she might like to work in, which suggested moving on was part of her mindset. He knew she'd originally been interested in being a naturalist, the kind of ranger who gave talks and happily staffed backcountry stations. She'd done that kind of thing for several summers, but getting taken on full time by the National Park Service wasn't easy. Eventually she'd attended the law enforcement academy at Skagit Valley College here in Washington state and gotten certified as an EMT and a structural firefighter as well. When an offer for a permanent position came, she jumped on it, even if it wasn't quite what she'd wanted in the first place.

He tended to keep things shallow when he was seeing a woman, but he had asked once if she regretted her choice or was still looking for a chance to shift away from the law enforcement track.

They'd been having lunch beside Lake Constance on their way to climb the mountain. With an oddly pensive expression, she'd glanced around at a beautiful spot that was undoubtedly once pristine, but had become almost as crowded as a park in Seattle in summer, and said, "The trouble is, it's gotten so all of us, no matter what our job title is, are mainly occupied protecting the land and animals from the visitors, and the visitors from each other and even from themselves."

He knew what she meant. She'd found a suicide victim the previous week and had to tell the man's fiancée about it. And it seemed as if half her time was spent on rescues involving climbers and hikers both. Too often the injured were people who hadn't prepared adequately for the outing they'd set out on.

That day, Cadence had given a one-shoulder shrug and said wryly, "There's not much time left over for anything else."

He could see her point. Spending time with her had given him insight into the challenges the national parks faced. The Grand Canyon, for example, was popular for anyone willing to commit suicide by jumping, with no thought given to the ugliness of the job rangers had cleaning up after what had likely been carefully planned acts. Yellowstone in particular had to contend with tourists who thought they ought to be able to set their kid on a buffalo's back for a picture or take a selfie with a grizzly. Here, tragedies on the beaches predominated, along with mountain rescue deep in a park that had virtually no road access.

He'd learned from her, as she had from him when he told her selective stories about policing a major city. What they hadn't done was share backgrounds. He knew she had parents and a brother who, while younger than her but still an adult, lived at home. No, he also knew that camping and traveling to scenic places had been part of her childhood, thus her interest in America's remaining wilderness areas.

The few mentions of her family had told him that she loved them. He hadn't caught a hint of resentment or distancing.

It went without saying that he'd kept quiet about his own childhood. Maybe she thought he'd been raised by his grandparents. If so, he hadn't corrected her.

What difference does it make? he asked himself now, angry at having to acknowledge his grandfather was right: having Cadence walk away from him had done a number on his mood. He needed to put her out of his mind, start looking for someone else who'd be satisfied with good sex and occasional companionship.

Too bad Garrett hadn't seen another woman who remotely interested him in months. Probably since he first set eyes on Cadence during a tricky traffic stop when she'd been his closest backup.

He swore under his breath. What could he do but accept her decision…however much he regretted it?

Putting a ring on her finger, turning now into forever, wasn't possible for a man who didn't believe he was capable of that kind of commitment—or that any woman would keep a commitment to *him*.

The urgency of a voice coming from his radio had him straightening. He was almost grateful for it.

A BLACK SUV driven by a man with a male passenger was spotted just north of Quilcene. When Deputy Herrera accelerated to close in behind it, the driver sped up in turn. Herrera turned on lights and siren—and the driver of the SUV must have slammed his gas pedal to the floorboards. By the time he flew by Garrett's position, the Tahoe—yes, Garrett recognized the lines—exceeded ninety miles an hour. It swerved around slower traffic in front of it; northbound vehicles fled for the shoulder.

God, Garrett didn't want to let it go, but he spoke up and said, "We need to abandon pursuit. I repeat, abandon pursuit. If we don't, we'll have a head-on collision any minute."

The sheriff came on. "All units, cease pursuit. Units farther south, watch for vehicle."

Garrett had gotten the license plate number and shared that on the radio. A state patrolman closer to Brinnon spoke up moments later. "Confirm license plate number. Black Tahoe just blew by me, but I don't believe the driver saw me off the road. He has slowed considerably. I estimate sixty-five to seventy miles per hour. I'll follow, but keep a distance."

Garrett drove only slightly over the speed limit to keep in touch. Other deputies farther south spoke up, as did deputies from the next county south.

"Saw me," a Jefferson County deputy said suddenly. "Vehicle is speeding up. Swerved and right wheels skidded in gravel."

"Hang back and watch only," the sheriff ordered.

It went on. Evidence of panic showed, which made the pursuit increasingly dangerous. The last deputy lost visual again. Last seen passing the turn to the Dosewallips Ranger Station, a dead end. Somewhere in the next few miles, the vehicle once more disappeared. They got lucky when a Mason County deputy reported a few minutes later that a motorist had stopped and pinpointed a forest service road also leading west, probably into the Brothers Wilderness area. He'd seen the SUV slamming on brakes and spinning and swerving off the road, raising a cloud of dirt that hung in its passage.

Yet another dead end, but this one was more complicated as the forest service roads in varying conditions intersected, and it would be possible to emerge back onto the highway farther south—or potentially north, although that seemed an unlikely choice on their part.

Once again, deputies were ordered into position. Half an hour later, it reemerged. Two deputies set up a roadblock.

"Shots fired!" one of them yelled. "Windshield is shattered." Garrett's heart damn near stopped as he continued driving. The sound was muted, but he could hear the *bang, bang, bang* of gunshots. "Returning fire! Aiming for a tire!" And then, "They're gone."

The men had once again fled the highway, but to Garrett's alarm, onto a road that actually went somewhere. Worse, to Lake Cushman, a long body of water outside the park boundary. In summer, scattered resorts, rentals and campgrounds would be full. The lake was easily accessible from Hoodsport on the canal—and from Olympia not that far south. The chances of disaster grew by the minute. In flashes behind his eyelids, Garrett saw a multivehicle accident, bodies thrown onto the pavement, or a hostage situation once the men realized that they were perilously close to being trapped. From Lake Cushman, there weren't many alternatives for escape, the principal one Highway 119.

This wouldn't have been his choice for where to draw the line, but he couldn't see that they had any options now. It was time for major roadblocks.

Fortunately, he didn't have to say a word. The sheriff would be looking at the same maps. He issued orders that would pen the two fugitives at Lake Cushman—along with far too many tourists.

Garrett had never been tenser

…until a man's voice took advantage of a break in radio traffic concerning the fugitives to identify himself as Ranger Chaffee with a report on a potential heart attack victim up the trail from the Staircase Ranger Station.

"Doing well with just oxygen. Ranger Jones and I are transporting the victim back down the Wagonwheel trail. Want to confirm request for an ambulance to meet us at the trailhead."

Ranger Jones.

The steering wheel creaked when Garrett's hands tightened. If Cadence and Chaffee reached that trailhead…there wasn't the slightest doubt she would jump right into the drama playing out so close to her current whereabouts.

Chapter Five

Sweating uncomfortably, Cadence especially regretted the necessity of wearing the broad-brimmed Stetson that immediately identified her as a park service employee. She currently anchored one corner of the wheeled gurney carrying a man in his seventies who'd become short of breath taking a particularly strenuous trail that left from the Staircase Ranger Station. After he collapsed, the youngest member of the party had run for help. Both the ranger on duty at Staircase—a likable, stocky man named Tom Chaffee—and Cadence had responded. The hiker had gotten farther than she'd have expected, reaching a stretch that required some bushwhacking on this return trip across an open avalanche slope.

She felt reasonably confident that the guy, who'd regained consciousness before she arrived, hadn't had a heart attack despite his admission that he'd previously had one. Lucky for him, given how long it would take to get him down to meet an ambulance.

"Angioplasty made me feel like a new man," he'd said breathlessly just before she fitted an oxygen mask over his face. He momentarily lifted it to add, "Guess I got too excited."

"There are a lot of hikes in the Olympics that I suspect you could take without difficulty," Cadence had said mildly. Ones that didn't require switchbacks because of the extreme elevation gain.

He wanted to walk down, but she and Tom agreed that was a nonstarter even though the steep descent meant carrying the fellow more than they could wheel him.

At the best of times, this wasn't one of her favorite hikes. The difficulty wasn't justified by the mostly limited views, although Wagonwheel Lake, a deep aquamarine color, was beautiful. This was one man who'd never see that particular lake, however.

Thankfully, both his sons—fit men—a daughter-in-law and two sons-in-law in their twenties had accompanied him. They had enough muscle-on-the-hoof to be able to take turns with hefting the gurney and preventing it taking off at a precipitous speed downhill.

Her attention wasn't 100 percent on doing her job. Nope, she was riveted by the radio traffic. During the shoot-out, she let one of the sons-in-law take her place so she could drop back and listen. Her body jerked involuntarily at the sound of shots. She could picture what was happening frighteningly well.

She stopped, letting the rest go on, as she absorbed the snapped orders and comments. Neither deputy had been seriously injured, but both were shaken. She'd encountered occasional Mason County sheriff's deputies on the job, but didn't recognize either of these names. She had the impression that one was young; his voice had been high and panicky at a moment experienced police officers maintained an unnatural calm.

The roadblock had accomplished one thing, however; the fleeing Tahoe had sped onto the offshoot, Highway 119, that ultimately met the graded gravel road that followed the shore of Lake Cushman…then entered the national park where it came to an end. At the Staircase campground. Where Cadence and her party would be appearing once they managed the steep descent, and where she hoped an ambulance would be waiting.

Surely to God the two killers would realize their mistake long before they reached the primitive campground, and turn around or try to find a way to go to ground. The tight band around her chest was a good reminder that they hadn't used any common sense yet, however, not from the very beginning when they chose an isolated gun shop in a rural county without many options to flee, when they thought gunning down a law enforcement officer would help their cause, or when they kept speeding down a narrow, scenic, too-busy highway even though they had seen or been briefly seen by a number of cops.

They had to be desperate by this time, grappling wildly for any way at all they might escape the disaster they had created.

Their most logical, if terrifying, option was to grab some hostages at Lake Cushman. Use those hostages to persuade law enforcement to let them drive on toward a city where they might still hope they could vanish—or, at the very least, to surrender safely.

She gazed after the party she needed to rejoin without really seeing them.

No, men still willing to shoot themselves out of trouble weren't thinking about surrender.

WHEN GARRETT AND another experienced deputy from Jefferson County paused briefly at the scene of the roadblock, nobody questioned their presence. These men had been listening to his voice for much of the day. No matter what, the manhunt had become multijurisdictional. Garrett's boss had talked about calling in the FBI in hopes they'd send the equivalent of a SWAT or Hostage Rescue Team to provide assistance. They were fast approaching that level of desperation.

He drove in a convoy with his coworker and two Mason County Sheriff's Department vehicles. Garrett had mostly stayed on paved roads thus far, while Deputy Dawes's vehicle was dust coated. They passed the Lake Cushman Golf Club and the beginnings of rustic businesses, including some that rented boats or offered small cabins for rent. They split up to search parking lots, short lanes leading to resorts or boat launches, the park. Garrett took responsibility for questioning people at the park.

Nothing.

Lake Cushman was magnificent—long and narrow, surrounded by steep, forested foothills. Right now, everything from kayaks to power boats were scattered across the lake. The view from the beach here in the park was impressive, although he barely gave it a passing glance.

Shouldn't somebody have noticed a speeding vehicle spitting gravel behind it as it headed for the park entrance? Garrett asked himself as he got back into his vehicle. Only, what if the Tahoe hadn't been speeding anymore? It was too late in the day for campers to be arriving at Staircase; the limited sites would already be full. But that didn't mean there wasn't still some traffic going that way. Maybe folks who just wanted a look at the river, the rapids, the bridge. Campers who had taken in other sites today. Tourists would have no reason to pay attention to other tourists, and locals? High summer was the equivalent of the biblical plague of locusts.

Damn it. He'd have to drive to the park entrance sta-

tion and be sure the fugitives hadn't fled to the very end
of the road.

"Someone appears to be holed up in an isolated house,"
came the voice of one of the MCSD deputies. "Landlord
came to clean up, because it's supposed to be vacant and
he has new renters due tomorrow. Door is barricaded and
he heard shouts."

"I'm on my way," he said, and on leaving the parking
lot turned back the way he'd come.

STILL DISTRACTED BY the heavy volume of traffic on the
radio, Cadence had to jog to catch up with the others. It
sounded as if events had descended into chaos. She was
ashamed to realize that what she was really listening for
was Garrett's voice or call signal. Naturally, he was still
in the middle of this.

She assumed she'd be joining the manhunt as soon as she
reached the foot of this infernal trail, but there was a ways
to go yet. She might not be to keep from worrying about
him, but that didn't mean she looked forward to seeing him.

Nearly an hour later, her group had reached a stretch
passing through a dry forest of young Douglas fir when
she heard a far-off scream.

They all stumbled to a stop, heads turning.

The second scream was thin and high, and moments
later was joined by more screams and voices yelling. Unless another group of hikers who were approaching had
just had a cataclysmic accident—and she couldn't imagine what that would be—she had to be hearing people at
the campground or trailhead. Cadence regretted suddenly
the ranger's insistence on accompanying her. If he'd been
there to intervene and report on what was happening—

Tom's eyes met hers. "I'll go—"

"No, I should." He didn't carry a gun, but did have the same EMT certification she did, which made him capable of continuing to monitor the health of their patient. "I'll radio you when I find out what's happening."

He looked like a horse straining to bolt, but nodded. "Go!"

One of the sons-in-law had been listening and now stepped forward to take her place. "We're down the worst part. Dad will be fine. *We'll* be fine."

God, she hoped so. She couldn't remember ever abandoning a person in distress to plunge into another crisis. She wouldn't have felt she *could* had Tom not been here.

She gripped the straps of the small pack and broke into a headlong run. Time seemed to both speed and slow down. What was *happening*? She had a sickening fear that it involved the two men who'd already killed once, but why would they have gotten themselves pinned at the edge of a vast wilderness? No, she realized: at a campground occupied by families.

She hadn't heard a gunshot. That was one blessing. But the closer she got, the more a babel of voices and the sobbing of a woman reached her.

Once she tripped over a root that snaked just beneath the dirt on the trail and had to do a dance to right herself. Under other circumstances, she'd have paused to catch her breath, but she couldn't. It was a huge relief to finally burst out on the paved path that led from the trailhead to the ranger station, then on to the campground where people were gathered. And, oh God, a seemingly empty, dusty black Tahoe sat askew in the middle of the circle road, blocking access to a campsite.

She hurried toward the crowd, raising her voice to make herself heard.

They engulfed her, men, women, teens. A few children peeked from tents or campers or clutched their parents' legs.

"I'm Park Ranger Jones," she said loudly. "Who can tell me what happened?"

They rushed into speech, talking over themselves, so that it was impossible to make out any coherent narrative. One woman kept sobbing like a metronome, in and out, in and out.

Cadence broke in. "Please, one at a time. You." She pointed to a man who'd been trying without success to get a word in edgewise.

"Two armed men jumped out of this SUV." He jerked his head toward it. "They waved guns. Slammed them into a few heads."

"What?" She looked around. "We have injured?"

"I don't think seriously."

At his nod indicating direction, she saw several men sitting on the dirt right off the road. One held his bent head between his hands. There were bruises, some blood, but nobody was dying.

"Okay." She had to lift her voice again over the din that had resumed. "Then what?"

Someone had started screaming the minute one of the men pointed a rifle at her. He yelled at her to shut up. The two had stood back to back, ordering everyone to stay put. Unfortunately, nobody had thought to try to slip away at the beginning. For what good that would have done, when they'd have found the ranger station empty.

A guy who looked to be about her age stepped forward.

"They wanted backpacks, insisted on meals for several days. The two of us—" he indicated a second man who stood beside him "—had already loaded up for an early morning departure. We intended to climb—" He swallowed. "I guess that doesn't matter. We nabbed a campsite because our wives and kids planned to wait for us here."

Cadence nodded her understanding.

"They took the packs. While one of them kept his gun on us, the other one poked around in both packs to be sure we weren't lying. When he seemed satisfied, we thought they'd take off, although…" He shook his head, his bafflement plain. "Where did they think they could *go*?"

There was the question.

She thought they deserved an answer. "A couple of men broke into a gun store up in Sequim early this morning. They killed a deputy who responded to the alarm. Every law enforcement agency in the area has been chasing them all day. I suspect it got too hot for them out on the highway, and they think they can slip away somehow in the park."

"Yes, but—" The climber jerked his shoulders. His gaze slid to the still crying woman. "They grabbed a kid and hauled him along."

Oh, dear God.

"Um, that's the boy's grandmother," he added.

"How old is the boy?"

"Eleven," said an older man beside the woman, his own face as blotchy as if he'd been crying earlier. "We brought our grandkids camping. Evan is eleven. Tall for his age, but…"

"All right." She did her best to sound confident, in charge. "Did anyone see which way they went?"

The second climber nodded. "I…followed a little ways. North Fork trail. They were moving fast, yanking the kid along. Man, if I'd been armed…"

"I looked in the back of their SUV," another man in the crowd called. "A tarp is covering the load, but an edge of it slid back enough I could see *piles* of weapons. We could break the windows and arm ourselves…"

Others were nodding, one saying loudly, "Let's do it!"

She backed up against that dusty fender and laid her hand on the butt of her sidearm. "I'll arrest the first person who takes a swing at a window. Do you hear me?"

They didn't like it, but they heard. Her gaze roved over the forty plus adults in the crowd. Probably most wouldn't have joined in forming a vigilante party, but a few were champing at the bit.

"Yeah, you going to take them down by yourself?" one was so bold as to ask.

"No. These are extremely dangerous men. They shot and wounded a store owner, killed a sheriff's deputy and opened fire on two other cops who set up a roadblock. I'll get on the radio and have backup here shortly. Law enforcement officers and *only* law enforcement officers will pursue those men on foot. We'll likely get a helicopter in the air to try to pinpoint where they are, in case they leave the trail. I need you to stay calm and give me any and all information you think might be useful."

Thank God none of these campers *had* been armed. Fortunately, carrying a gun of any kind wasn't allowed in the national parks, and apparently no one in this crowd had tried to slip one by. If so, it wouldn't have been a shock; she'd issued many a citation to would-be hunters who didn't respect park rules, or just men who needed the swagger carrying gave them.

"He wanted a map," a woman said, stepping forward. "I'd just been looking at that one I picked up at the ranger station. It shows trails throughout the park. I…handed them that."

"That's good to know." The map in question didn't have

the scope and detail of the larger topographic map put out by *National Geographic*, but she wasn't sure that mattered. "Okay, let me make my call."

Some people shuffled off toward their campsites. Others seemed to need to talk, but she tuned them out, giving her call sign and saying, "The fugitives who burglarized the gun shop and have been pursued all day drove into Staircase campground in the national park. They left behind their black Tahoe." She gave the license plate number. "Heavily armed, they have fled on foot deeper into the park, taking an older child hostage with them. They've now had as much as an hour head start. I need armed searchers carrying what they'll need for potentially two to three days. We all know there's a lot of country out there they can get lost in." She paused. "Please respond."

LISTENING, GARRETT COULD have sworn the hair on his arms stood on end as if he'd been electrified. He'd been apprehensive before—during last week's traffic stop, for example—but scared like this? Not even at the worst moments in foster care.

She's okay, he told himself. It didn't sound as if she'd seen them, much less confronted them. That should have been some comfort, but she would definitely be among the group heading deep into the park to find two men who had nothing to lose at this point.

This intense reaction alarmed him. Where had it come from? Yeah, he'd missed her, but he'd move on eventually. That's what he did. No, this was just his protective instinct, a big part of him. On some level, she'd been *his*, and even if that relationship proved to be temporary, he couldn't turn off this fear for her…or the certainty that his primary goal now was keeping her safe.

He leaped back into his SUV, leaving two deputies to extract what appeared to be squatters from a rental house, and exploded back onto North Lake Cushman Road. He raced past the park entry, noted a couple of ranger vehicles parked by the station as well as an ambulance that had somehow beat him here. Entering the campground circle, he immediately zeroed in on the too-familiar Tahoe. It wasn't so much parked as abandoned where the driver had slammed on his brakes.

Two medics appeared to be looking over a few battered men. Amongst the clusters of agitated people, Garrett didn't immediately see Cadence. She wouldn't have gone in pursuit on her own, would she? He wouldn't believe that. She could be reckless, but—

He was suddenly able to breathe. There she was, crouched with an arm around a distraught older woman who sat in a lawn chair someone had carried almost to the road for her. Garrett had seen compassion on Cadence's fine-boned face before, but he was inexplicably surprised by it anyway. As fit as she was, she'd just loaded herself up with medical supplies and hiked—or jogged—almost to Wagonwheel Lake, an elevation gain of at least 3,000 feet. She'd treated a man with heart trouble, then despite her slight body, helped carry him most of the way down on a gurney—until she'd rushed headlong down to the campground. There, she'd been met by a lot of upset people who still milled around.

And, yeah, he saw sweat circles under her arms, a dirty streak on her face, and her usually smooth dark hair was escaping a braid with one especially long strand that she pushed impatiently back behind her ear. Yet she was still herself, every movement graceful even as she remained composed and yet exuding warmth for a deeply distressed woman.

Cadence's head turned just then, and her dark eyes locked onto his. Whether he liked it or not, his heart gave a hard squeeze. The relief on her face eased his tumult, and he walked toward her. She never looked away.

"Can we talk?" he said.

"Of course." She murmured something to the woman, gave her a hug and then rose to her feet, coming toward him. Her Kevlar vest only emphasized how willowy her build was. She might be delicately made, but she was stronger than anyone first meeting her would suspect. He'd climbed and hiked with her enough to know just how fit and capable she was.

Sounding anxious, she said, "We need to get going as soon as possible. What are you hearing?"

"The license plate was stolen off another vehicle, to no one's surprise, but once the techs lift some fingerprints from the Tahoe, I'm betting there'll be matches."

She only nodded, and he understood why she wasn't excited. Identifying the men didn't help right now.

"We'll have two other teams besides ourselves ready to go within another hour, hour and a half," Garrett continued. "Everyone had to hustle home to grab their backpacks and supplies. We might still add another team before nightfall. Others will set out in the morning."

"Morning." She sounded almost numb.

"You know we'll be unlikely to catch up to them tonight."

"We're in good shape!" she cried. "They may not be."

"They may not be runners, but from the footage I saw, they have to be weight lifters and maybe use machines in a gym. Or box or—" He stopped. "We can't assume they'll be slow."

"I know, but..."

"Cadence." He made sure she met his eyes. "In the morning, we'll send in searchers from other directions. Up the Duckabush River, for example, and maybe the Dose, since the trails all connect. It's too late in the day to get a helicopter in the air, but I know the air force base is prepared to send one in the morning."

She was breathing harder than he'd seen her yet. He made an involuntary move toward her that she didn't seem to notice, but made himself stop, his hands fisting at his sides. They couldn't be seen wrapped in each other's arms in front of a campground full of frightened tourists—assuming she'd have let him gather her to him.

"It's the boy," she said so softly he just heard her. "He's only eleven. He must be petrified."

"Yeah," he said regretfully. "I know." He'd been trying not think about the poor kid, or what his captors would do with him if he couldn't keep up with them or was foolish enough to try to make a break for it.

He did take her hand and gave it a quick squeeze. To his relief, her fingers tightened on his, if only momentarily. Had she realized from what he said that he fully intended to pair up with her? If so, she wasn't arguing, thank God.

Lucky, because he wasn't taking no for an answer—not about this, not from her. After all the shocks of the day, he had some thinking to do. What he knew right now was that he wouldn't be able to do his job if he couldn't have her as close as possible.

Chapter Six

The brief touch of his hand reignited her wariness. Getting over him meant rebuffing any hint of tenderness. She deliberately raised her chin. "What about you? You surely don't carry your pack around."

He'd know that she did.

"My grandfather is meeting Deputy McCall, who has a young woman deputy with him. I don't know her well. They're both outfitted."

"Alysa Bailey? I've met her. She talked about competing in a triathlon."

"Excellent. Two Mason County deputies are on their way, too—both say they're climbers and know this part of the park well. That'll give us six to start out. I'm told the park ranger is organizing people, but since you're the best informed, he's leaving you in charge for now."

She'd half expected him to argue, not so much because he was male and she was female as because taking charge came naturally to him. But obviously he recognized that they were now in her jurisdiction, and in territory she knew better than he did.

"I had a call from him," she agreed.

"I took the liberty of setting up what I could," Garrett continued. "If you disagree…"

"No." She tried a smile that didn't quite make it. "I'm grateful. I...hadn't gotten that far in my thinking yet. You have no idea how much I wanted to charge after them, but at least I knew better than to do that."

"I was glad to see you," he said abruptly, something odd in his tone.

She raised her eyebrows. "Because you thought I might go ahead on my own."

"No, you said you wouldn't." He cleared his throat. "But waiting isn't always the easiest thing to do."

"No." She sighed and told him that half the men in the crowd would be thrilled to be issued weapons so they could join the manhunt. She was reasonably sure she'd squelched the surge of volunteerism, but was still keeping an eye on the ringleaders. "By the way, as one of them pointed out, it appears there are plenty of weapons in the back of the Tahoe."

"They're not covered?" he asked in surprise.

"There's a tarp, but it may have slipped during their high-speed maneuvering. Either that, or they grabbed some weapons from the back. I hope you have someone coming to secure the vehicle and contents?"

"Yeah, a park special agent is on his way along with a Clallam County detective, since the original crime was theirs and the weapons will eventually be returned to the gun shop owner."

"Oh, right." Her head turned sharply. "Some reinforcements."

The driver was wedging his department vehicle off the road to the best of his ability. Garrett said, "Those are the Mason County guys. You might want to talk to them. I met one of them earlier." He grimaced. "I'll guard the stockpile here."

Oh, yeah. Good idea. She nodded and went to meet the two men who had the back of their official vehicle open and were swinging packs out onto their backs. One had salt-and-pepper hair. She'd guess him to be in his upper forties or even fifties, but he was lean and fit. The second deputy was probably around her age, more powerfully built. That wasn't necessarily an advantage for what lay ahead of them, but she wouldn't judge ahead of his performance.

She introduced herself, and they did the same. The older man was Eric Sutherland, the younger Tyler Murray. She decided their vehicle could stay where it was, then sent them on to join Garrett while she jogged back to the ranger station to update Tom Chaffee.

"Hell of a day," he said, on seeing her. "Ambulance just left. Our patient looked good. I suspect he'll be released this evening. The medics decided to take one of the campers who got slammed with a rifle butt, too. They suspect a concussion."

The one clutching his head, Cadence presumed.

Tom raised his eyebrows. "I assume you're going in pursuit."

She nodded. "I need to grab my pack out of my car."

He asked about the SUV full of stolen weapons and was obviously relieved to hear people were on their way to take charge of it.

"I put a Closed sign at the entrance. There's no space at the campground, anyway, and we don't need any gawkers."

"No." She hesitated. "You stay sharp. It's unlikely those two men can figure out how to loop back here, but they may be thinking they can. Even if they can't recover their Tahoe, hey, point a gun at some campers and steal *their* car."

"I'll have an eye out," he agreed. "Keep us informed."

"Will do." She smiled crookedly. "The kid's grandparents are site number eight. You might stop by and reassure them."

"Had that in mind."

She pawed through her own pack briefly, adding additional medical supplies from the bag she'd carried earlier and discarding a few extras before closing fasteners once she was satisfied. Then she took her M16 rifle from the rack, stuck extra ammunition for it and her handgun in outside pockets of her pack and heaved it experimentally onto her back. Heavier than usual, but fine, she decided, and carried it to rejoin the others.

Unbelievable. Six of them were to plunge into the park to track and eventually attempt to subdue men who were probably better armed than the pursuers. Men who'd already displayed their willingness to kill. She hoped her compatriots were dedicated enough to put in regular time at the range to stay sharp.

Let us recover the boy, she begged, before bullets start flying.

CADENCE WASN'T HIDING her impatience well, although Garrett couldn't blame her. These things always dragged on for a frustrating length of time.

A month ago, Garrett and Cadence had hiked the beginning of this trail but detoured to have lunch at Flapjack Lakes before turning back. He seemed to remember that she'd hiked most of it—maybe cutting over to Enchanted Valley—but Garrett hadn't. Now he carefully studied the map she pinned to the bole of a tree with one hand.

"Unless it looks like someone set out cross-country, we'll stick together until here." With a glance around, she pointed at the trail that wound to Flapjack Lakes and beyond, to Mount Cruiser, a tough rock climb Garrett hadn't yet attempted. Unfortunately, that same trail had at least one other branch leading to a series of lakes as well as a more primitive track that met the main North Fork trail at a campsite called Big Log that he and she would pass in a few hours. "At least one pair should split off there. If we had more people, I'd say two pairs, but once we reach the Big Log spur, which continues along Six Ridge, we'll need to explore that possibility, too."

Garrett agreed with her reasoning, and saw that the others did, too. Since the Six Ridge trail meandered south toward the national park border, it might seem like a good option to men desperate for a way out.

"Remember," she added, "you need to watch for game trails and unmarked trails used by climbers or backpackers wanting to set up camp off the beaten path. Even trails made by animals. You'll see plenty of them."

More nods.

"That brings us to the subject of how we should pair up," she said, as if it had just occurred to her. Her gaze didn't meet Garrett's. "If anyone has a particular strength or weakness—"

He interrupted without apology. "It seems to me we should pair with the person we know best and have worked with before. It's important we can read each other in a tight spot and know how our partner will react."

Her mouth tightened.

The older of the two Mason County deputies said, "I agree. It might be different if we had a larger group to organize, but as it is, we arrived two by two. Why don't we keep it that way?"

He could tell she didn't like that, but nodded curtly. The others—well, except for the Jefferson County duo—couldn't possibly guess that he and Cadence had been sleeping together and recently parted ways, that there were some touchy feelings between them. But he trusted her skill, and thought she did his. They couldn't let those feelings get in the way of rescuing the young hostage.

"What if we spot them?" asked Deputy Bailey.

"That depends on whether they see *you*," Cadence said. "If possible, radio in the sighting first. Keep in mind that the safety of the hostage has to be our priority. If you find yourself under fire... Backing off might be the best tactic until we can overwhelm them with numbers."

"We're lucky this is Tuesday," Garrett commented. "The weekend running into Monday would have been the most crowded up here, but even so we have to assume they will meet other people out on the trail."

Eric Sutherland pointed out, "There's not much we can do about that. Let's just hope people use their common sense, and that our fugitives aren't too trigger-happy."

Garrett's jaw tightened. He could see any number of possible bad outcomes when a party of climbers, say, came around a bend in the trail to find themselves face-to-face with men toting forbidden automatic rifles.

They threw around a few more thoughts, Cadence all but dancing in place from anxiety and impatience. Understanding, Garrett suggested he and she as well as the two Mason County deputies set out now, while the Jefferson County pair hung around until someone arrived to take responsibility for the Tahoe and its cache of weapons.

Cadence assigned those two, once they were able to get moving, to take the trail to Flapjack Lakes as well as the dogleg to Smith Lake. "It's not much over three miles to reach that turnoff," she said. Given how late it's getting, you might want to set up camp right at the junction." She looked around at all of them. "It probably goes without saying, but use flashlights as little as possible. You won't want to pinpoint your location."

By the time the foursome set out on what had originally been a generously wide road grade, it was with the knowledge that the light would start failing in just a couple of hours. They didn't dare continue in the dark for a number of reasons, but the big one was that they might miss seeing evidence that the men had left the trail.

Ian Sutherland and Tyler Murray fell in behind Garrett and Cadence, both appearing comfortable carrying the heavy packs and weapons, their strides long and relaxed. Garrett saw that Cadence was surreptitiously checking them out, too, her forehead smoothing when she turned her focus onto the trail ahead.

They'd walked for fifteen minutes, the rippling sound of the river accompanying them, before she said, voice low but intense. "I *hate* that we let them get so far ahead of us."

Feeling a stir of the same anger, he said, "I don't blame you. We've had no choice but to react to these SOBs all day long. Not my favorite position to be put into. The one time we got in front of them, we didn't have enough force in place to stop them. In retrospect, I don't know how smart it was to set up that roadblock, given that it took every option away from them but this one."

"Yes, but their chances of disappearing with the stolen weapons would have been greater once they reached urban areas."

He grunted. "There's a lot of miles out here to get lost in."

She gave something like a shudder. "They could get lost with my blessing, if only they hadn't grabbed the boy."

Except they would have had access to other hostages if they needed a replacement. Garrett didn't say that.

"I think we can assume that we'll be able to move faster than they will." He went for calm. "By tomorrow, we'll have a full-blown manhunt in place, including eyes in the sky."

"Which may or may not do any good, considering much of the time anyone out here will be hidden by lush forest."

He shrugged his concession, guessing she'd see him out of the corner of her eye. He thought about bringing up the subject of their pairing, but decided not to. He'd have dug in his heels even if the logic behind the decision hadn't been so compelling, but she didn't know that. If she was angry enough at him to have trouble working cooperatively, he might regret his insistence, but he didn't think so.

"Take it easy," he said, after a minute. "You're all but running." He kept up with his longer stride, but had to push a little. She knew better than to take a chance of injuring herself by starting too hard and fast.

She shot him a dark look, but did slow down to a more natural, steady pace.

The two behind them were chatting, but quietly. He noted places where a tree had fallen over the trail, but crews had sawed through to clear the way. Cadence didn't even pause when they reached a viewpoint above the river. That was fine, but they needed to make sure they weren't walking right by some trampled vegetation or other indication that people ahead of them had set off cross-country. He suggested she be responsible for scanning to the left, him to the right.

She bit her lip. "I doubt they'd leave the trail this soon, but…you're right. That's a good idea."

He started watching more carefully for any small indication that someone had stepped off the trail—broken undergrowth, a boot print, scuffed soil—even as he kept more of an eye on her than she'd like. They'd been equal partners when climbing; he'd never had any doubt that, with her on the other end of the rope, he didn't have to worry. He probably wouldn't be in the profession he was if he didn't have a need to protect, but it wasn't usually so powerful, or so focused on a woman who wasn't actually in danger.

At the moment, he reminded himself, not liking the idea that the two of them could come unexpectedly on those bastards. The tension that squeezed in his chest made him think it was just as well she *had* ditched him. Feeling this way wasn't comfortable. It was part of what he'd been determined to avoid by keeping his friendships and involvement with women shallow.

After a couple of miles, the trail narrowed enough they needed to go single file much of the time, taking a gradual downward trend that led them into the lush forest. Now and again they had to step over horse droppings, this being one of the trails in the park where horses were not only permitted, but accommodated with corrals.

Sunlight became diffused, filtering through the needles and lacy branches of ancient Douglas fir, cedar and hemlock rearing high above them. Any opening in the canopy had been filled by maple trees. Moss draped over vines, ferns and other undergrowth made this a world of dozens of shades of green. The temperate rainforest on the western side of the park might be more spectacular, with lichens draping from branches like tinsel on a Christmas tree, but this section was magnificent in its own right, and all too rare. Thanks to Cadence, Garrett knew that the park sheltered 250,000 acres of old-growth forest, while, thanks to logging and human-caused fires, only a tiny percent remained outside those boundaries. He'd read that Douglas fir this size could be a thousand years old, or more. Planting replacement trees didn't cut it. The land protected by the park wasn't just to be appreciated for its beauty, the diverse forest was a resource for the future.

He was disturbed to realize how dry the forest looked right now. Moss shouldn't be brown. He hadn't noticed at first, but his eye became more discerning. The small streams they crossed ran low enough, there was no danger of anyone getting wet. A good rain would help, but with the driest months of the year coming they'd mostly see drizzle.

The two behind them had quit talking. Garrett would have felt the weight of the silence, except complete silence was rare in the backcountry. A breeze stirred branches in the upper canopy, water burbled in the distance, birds called. An occasional rustle in the underbrush would turn his head until he was certain it had been caused by wildlife and not a crouched human being.

He thought all of them felt the uneasy prickle of awareness that they could be watched through powerful rifle scopes. No, it wasn't likely, given the density of the vegetation and the breadth of the trunks of these old-growth trees, but he couldn't rule out the possibility that armed men might decide to pick off any pursuers.

Garrett was suddenly glad of his Kevlar vest, and that Cadence wore one as well, as did the other deputies and every other individual who would set out to hunt a pair of cop killers.

CADENCE WAS AWARE of every feature along the trail that gave her a good guess at how far they'd come and what lay ahead. The forest changed, and they entered an impressive stand of big-leaf maple. Slate Creek was a warning of what lay ahead: a burned landscape that encompassed more than 1,300 acres. The Beaver Fire had been set many years ago by an illegal campfire, and she always found it shocking to see how far the land still had to go to regenerate. Shrubs had popped up first, then quick-growing deciduous trees from seeds dropped by birds or wafted by winds. Small firs, cedars and hemlock gave hope for a return to the forest that had once covered this land, and would again, even if so long in the future no one living now would see it. The blackened skeletons of forest giants reared above, warning of how easily this could happen anywhere. Cadence always thought about these sad remnants when she cited campers and backpackers for illegal fires. So few people understood how fast a flame could get away from them, how dangerous a few cinders glowing against the darkness could be if they found dry tinder.

"I don't like us being so out in the open," Garrett said abruptly, the first words he'd spoken in ages. She glanced at him to see him scanning their surroundings, tension in his bearing.

"Places like this almost make me a believer in ghosts," she heard herself say. "Not necessarily human, but..." She shrugged.

She felt his gaze touch on her, but he didn't comment, certainly didn't reason with her by pointing out that massive fires were a part of the ecosystem in any forest. She wouldn't disagree with that viewpoint, but *this* fire hadn't had to happen. Humans were so careless.

The two behind them murmured, voices low enough she couldn't hear what they said.

They all noted without comment the trail that cut away to the east that the Jefferson County deputies would take. As they hiked on, she became increasingly conscious of the deepening light as dusk crept toward them. The valley pinched, the trail they followed carved on a hillside above the rivers and streams that flowed at the narrowest point.

Places like this descended into darkness long before the orange orb of the sun sank behind the curve of the earth out over the ocean.

Maybe unconsciously, she and Garrett stepped up the pace, the others staying with them. A few times, they paused to check out signs of a faint trail to one side or the other. Most led to a riverside spot where hikers had paused for a snack or to splash water on their faces. Others were clearly animal trails. Cadence kept a sharp eye out for bears, which were commonly seen in the area, but didn't see much in the way of wildlife at all. The call of a grouse was the sum total. A mile and a half later, give or take, they spotted the designated campsite called Big Log, presently dotted by a half dozen tents. Funny they hadn't already met hikers on their last leg to the trailhead. Her uneasiness increased now that she'd consciously realized why she'd been so aware her small party was completely alone.

She stopped. "We need to find out if anyone saw who passed."

They split up, each taking one or two of the parties or individuals. Turned out, only one couple had paid any attention to a threesome that passed what might be a couple of hours ago.

"I'd have sworn they were carrying rifles," said the young woman. "But I didn't have any way to report them—" cell phone service was rare in the park "—and I didn't see them that closely."

"Any idea whether they continued north or headed toward Six Ridge?"

"I'm sorry, I wish I had."

"Okay." Cadence raised her voice so that everyone present could hear them. "It should be fine to stay here tonight, and to hike back to Staircase in the morning. If any of you were planning to continue on—"

Two men were.

"This area of the park has been closed because of the men you just heard us talking about," she told them. "I'm afraid I have to ask you to go with everyone else back to Staircase in the morning." She suggested they talk to the ranger there, who might be able to redirect them to another area of the park where they could hike or climb instead.

They didn't look happy, but they'd heard the mention of rifles and could see that Cadence and the three men with her were also armed and wearing police vests.

After thanking them for their cooperation and accepting their promises to pass on the information to any late arrivals, she and the others continued over a pack bridge that crossed the North Fork Skokomish River. Usually she savored the view here of the river passing through what was nearly a gorge, but today she was blind to scenery.

The trail she and Garrett would follow continued north on the eastern bank of the river now. Here was the cutoff for the Six Ridge trail that Ian and Tyler were to take. For the moment, though, they continued together, passing the site of an old mine that had been worked for copper, iron and manganese around the turn of the twentieth century, and on to Camp Pleasant, which turned out to be more occupied. Two horses drowsed in the corral. If the men and boy had been seen continuing north along the river, well, then maybe she wouldn't have to split her forces.

And, oh yes, be alone with Garrett for who knew how many days. The man who deserved to know she was carrying his baby.

Chapter Seven

Cadence had continued monitoring her radio, as she felt sure the others were. She was relieved when Ed McCall, one of Garrett's coworkers, reported that they had passed off custody of the Tahoe and its contents at last and were on their way.

"Should make the junction before dark," Ed added.

She confirmed she'd heard. "Copy."

Cadence knew she might be wasting the time of two members of her small team since she now had confirmation the men had fled with their hostage well past the Flapjack Lakes turnoff, but they could certainly circle back to those lakes from the Big Log campground, and chances were good there'd be other ways for them to cross the North Fork Skokomish River and go cross-country to join the very trail she'd assigned to Alyssa and Ed. No, she couldn't afford to ignore any possibility. Given the popularity of Mount Cruiser and surrounding peaks, she'd be willing to bet there were any number of tracks that might tempt fugitives to think they could evade their pursuers.

While she spoke briefly to Ed, Garrett had stayed close to her, but Ian and Tyler had gathered the campers and begun questioning them.

Cadence joined them just as a man stepped forward.

She was very conscious of Garrett sticking to her side, his upper arm brushing hers.

"Yeah, the four of us—" the man gestured to a couple of other men and a woman "—are planning to climb O'Neil Peak tomorrow. We got a later start than we'd meant to from Seattle, ran into traffic—you know how it is. Anyway, we'd almost reached the bridge back there when these two men and a kid came up from behind us. They seemed to be in an almighty hurry."

"I thought we were going to get run off the trail," one of the men commented.

"We waved them on—" said the first guy.

"I was about to ask if they knew guns weren't allowed in the park when Tony here elbowed me," said the third man.

Tony was apparently the original man who'd spoken up. "Figured we'd report them when we got down," he said. "Uh…even though that wouldn't have been a couple of days from now."

"The boy worried me," the woman said, voice soft. "He looked… I don't know."

Scared, Cadence thought. That's what he'd looked.

"You did the right thing to keep it casual and let them go on," she said. "They're dangerous men."

The woman's dismay was apparent. "The boy?"

"A hostage," Garrett told them bluntly. "That's one of the reasons we've launched a manhunt. I hope you can tell us which way they went."

"Which way? Oh, you mean Six Ridge or north?" That was the original speaker. "We kind of stopped and huddled. You know. Because they gave off such a weird vibe. We didn't want to get near them again." His mouth twisted. "I didn't see what they did once they were over the river."

None of them had. Cadence wanted to scream. Having

witnesses that could have narrowed their search area but decided *not* to see was frustrating. And yet, in being cautious they'd made the right call again.

Her hope wasn't entirely dead, but as it turned out, not a single soul who had earlier set up camp had paid any attention to other hikers coming or going on the trail.

A chorus of voices gave perfectly valid excuses. "I mean, I know there were some, but I was trying to figure out how to work my new stove."

"We walked over to look at the mine."

"People were partying at the state campground last night. I napped for a little while once we'd set up here."

Doing her absolute best to mask her frustration, Cadence gave the same instructions to this group, and the party that had intended to climb O'Neil Peak tomorrow didn't argue. She did get some kickback from two young guys who wanted to know if they could cut over on the Flapjack Lakes trail—or cross-country—to Mount Gladys and Mount Cruiser to climb tomorrow instead of continuing north to their original goal.

"No, I'm sorry." She made damn sure they could tell she meant it. "This entire area of the park is closed." Seeing that one was about to open his mouth, she said, "If you can detour that way, so can they. Don't provide them with another hostage."

That seemed to get through to them, possibly reinforced by Garrett's commanding stare. He definitely had the gift of stopping people dead with one hard look.

She, Garrett and the two Mason County deputies retreated.

"We'll split off now," Ian Sutherland said.

If only *someone* had seen which way the two gun-toting men with the frightened boy had gone. Since nobody had,

Cadence was left with no choice but to send two of her small search party on the initially steep trail to reach Six Ridge and ultimately leave the park and connect with some forest service roads.

That left her and Garrett to continue the pursuit north.

"I'd hoped we could eliminate that possibility, but since we can't…"

Ian only nodded. "We might spend the night at Big Log."

She didn't even have to glance up to know the color of the sky was deepening. Features were becoming subtly less distinct.

"Good. Stay in touch," she said.

The two swung packs onto their backs again and strode back the way they'd come.

"We could stay here," Garrett said into the silence.

That made sense; of course it did. There were reasons the Park Service normally allowed camping only in designated sites. In this case…there were primitive toilets here, which was a big plus.

Garrett saw something on her face and said gently, "I'm sure we can find a place to set up just off the trail."

She heard herself make a sound even she couldn't have named. "Let me make a pit stop first."

Literally, as it happened. They took turns, the brightness of the day diminishing even in that short time.

"We should stay."

"Your call," he said, with that same careful lack of pressure.

Her shoulders sagged. "Let's grab a spot close to the trail."

He smiled at her. "We wouldn't have gotten much farther."

"I know."

They chose a site sheltered by old conifers that was near to both the trail and the river.

"One tent or two?" he asked, as he set down his pack and undid straps.

Oh, heavens. It was silly to set up both tents when they'd shared one so often. In the interests of speed and doing as little damage as possible to native vegetation, they probably wouldn't be able to each have their own after this, not unless they were able to conveniently stop each night at other designated campsites. On the other hand…could she sleep inches away from the man she loved, the same man who'd shrugged and made clear he didn't feel anything close to the same for her?

GARRETT WAITED, feeling new tension. He'd sleep better to have her close. He didn't like the idea of tent walls separating them, of him potentially not hearing someone approach or her slipping out of her own tent. But he was painfully aware he had no right to push.

"One's fine," she said finally, "as long as it's clear the tent is *all* we share."

He hid the irritation that spiked and said, "I get it."

Without asking, he set up his slightly roomier tent, then tossed his pad and rolled sleeping bag inside. While he was doing that, she got the stove going and chose a couple of packets of freeze-dried… He couldn't make out the handwritten labels, but trusted her on this. She freeze-dried her own meals instead of buying them from outfitters the way he did.

Seeing what she was doing, he crouched to spread both their pads and sleeping bags with a noticeable gap between them, then lowered himself to sit on an upended log.

"We should start at first light." She mostly had her back to him, but Garrett could tell she was aware of his every move.

Of course they would.

They ate with near silence between them, but other voices and the soft gurgles and splashes of the river prevented some of the awkwardness that they might otherwise have felt. He was aware of regret, though, and what might even have been grief. During their backcountry trips, he had enjoyed their talks, wandering unpredictably from exchanges about their jobs to politics, ethical dilemmas, philosophy…anything and everything except family and how they felt. He flat out loved her voice, coming from the darkness. Faint huskiness had made him think about the night to come, when they'd be tangled together on top of their sleeping bags, Cadence crying out as she clutched him, Garrett pushing into her exquisitely tight body…

Damn it, damn it, damn it. His body had reacted instantly to his vision. Lucky the darkness and lack of a fire would keep her from noticing.

He let his body know it wasn't getting what it wanted and did the minimal cleanup, while she got on the radio and responded to the chief ranger about tomorrow's plans.

When she was done, she asked, "You heard all that?"

"I did. I wish they'd been able to muster a second helicopter, but one may be enough."

She made a frustrated sound. "I just keep thinking… what happens when we do see them? Worse yet, what if it's sudden?"

"I don't love having us spread so thin," he admitted. Major understatement. "It's too much like today's fiasco. As you said, though, we've got to get the boy away from them."

She released a shuddery breath that made him want to reach for her. He actually started to before forcing himself to stay where he was.

"Everyone knows that's their priority." He didn't really need to say that, but knew she needed to hear it anyway.

Stirring, Cadence said after a minute, "I'm not really sleepy, but I know dawn isn't that far away."

Days were exceptionally long in the northwest at this time of year. The longest day of the year was near, in fact, the summer solstice. That gave them more daylight and chance to hunt down these bastards, but the downside was that the men could more easily stay on the move, too.

He grunted his agreement and reached over his head to stretch, hearing a faint crack or two, appreciating the effect on his muscles. "If I have to tell people to shut up, I will."

She gave a choked laugh. "If either of us has to do that, it should be me. And really…nobody is being that loud."

He cocked his head. She was right. In fact, the hum of voices seemed unusually subdued to him. The people camping here must be feeling uncomfortably vulnerable. Yeah, he doubted any of these folks would make a late night of it. Most would be fleeing down the trail as early as they could be ready come morning.

"Maybe we should commandeer those horses," he suggested, not serious.

Instead of laughing, she said thoughtfully, "Maybe we should. Think how fast we could move."

"Uh-huh. One problem: I've never been on a horse in my life."

"You're kidding!"

"Nope. City boy. And problem number two—did you see the couple who got here on horseback?" They looked to be in their fifties, weathered skin, the guy with a belly starting to inch over his belt, the woman tiny and so fine boned, he hoped doctors were checking her bone density. Cowboy boots that would raise blisters in the first half hour of hiking. Backpackers, they weren't.

"Yeah, yeah." She huffed. "I didn't mean it."

"I know." Both were keeping their voices low, creating a sense of intimacy. He'd sounded…he didn't know, just that it made him uneasy. "Let's hit the sack," he said abruptly.

"Sure." She popped to her feet and gestured. "I'm going to use the facilities again."

"Me, too," he agreed, "but I'll wait until you get back." They couldn't leave their rifles and handguns unprotected.

What moon had risen was barely past a crescent and didn't offer enough light for him to watch Cadence for more than a few steps. When she vanished in the darkness, he tensed, eyes fixed on where she'd reappear. *For God's sake*, he thought, but couldn't make himself do anything but listen hard for a sound that was out of place, for her voice, for her footsteps.

Her voice he heard a few minutes later. She obviously stopped to reassure several sets of campers before materializing in front of him.

"Your turn."

As he could have predicted, she must have stripped in record time. By the time he got back, she was already in her sleeping bag, curled up with her back to him. Probably a smart move on her part, he conceded, avoiding the awkwardness of them bumping into each other as they peeled off tops, set boots aside and actually maneuvered into the side-by-side bags.

He wadded up his fleece quarter zip, figuring it was as good as he'd get for a pillow, laid his cargo pants aside and maneuvered into his own sleeping bag, all the while conscious of her so close. Cadence didn't move enough to cause even a faint rustle. Was she breathing? He gritted his teeth, forcing himself to think about what lay ahead of them.

Sunrise would come barely after 5:00 a.m. this time of year. Without cell phone service, they had no way to set an alarm, but he knew he'd have no trouble waking up, and Cadence was probably the same.

After an early start this morning and the stresses of the day, he should have been beat, but tell his brain that. He couldn't turn it off. Mostly, he couldn't prevent himself from remembering all the other times he'd shared a tent with Cadence.

He lay as still as he could, able to tell she was doing the same. Finally, he said aloud, "Hell! Neither of us will get any sleep." He reached for her. When he tugged, she rolled, her head finding his shoulder and his arm closing securely around her.

She fought. "What are you *doing*? You promised."

"I'm trying to get comfortable enough to sleep. That won't happen while we're lying here as rigid as a pair of mummies!"

"Speak for yourself!"

Conscious of other campers, he murmured, "Shhh."

She quit struggling, but said from between her teeth, "I was fine."

"I wasn't. But suit yourself." Closing his eyes, he deliberately relaxed the arm that encircled her and waited to see what she'd do.

The seconds stretched into a minute. Maybe two. Then she sighed and relaxed.

In the darkness, Garrett smiled. Unfortunately, his erection took too damn long to subside enough to let *him* sleep.

MORE COMFORTABLE THAN she would have wanted to admit to Garrett, Cadence knew she had even less chance of sleeping anytime soon. Well, she'd have been unlikely to, anyway. Her thoughts raced as she reran the day's events, her every decision, the decisions *everyone* had made. If only the pair had been stopped before they reached a trailhead. Worse yet, a trailhead near a campground full of people easy to intimidate. The last thing anyone coming to one of the most beautiful national parks expected was violence.

A part of her wished the grandmother hadn't showed her the photo on her phone of her grandson. Being able to picture Evan's face didn't help. Eleven years old, Grandma had said, but he was still skinny in the way of a boy just a few years away from puberty. The only hope Cadence held was that, according to Grandpa, Evan played soccer at a high level. Surely that meant he was in good shape…and fast, if he got the chance to run. The kid had brown hair, brown or hazel eyes and an infectious grin.

Hold on, she thought. *We're coming.*

That circled her back around to her worry about her and Garrett alone confronting men so brutally willing to use violence and even kill.

They could call in help.

But what would happen to Evan if the men knew they were cornered?

Out of the darkness came a husky murmur, "Easy." He squeezed her, just a brief tightening of his arm.

Was her body so stiff he'd been able to tell how tense she was? She made a face. Probably. Okay. Deep breath. Let it out. Another one. She imagined herself in a yoga class, lying on a mat, eyes closed, listening to her instructor.

Except in one way this was better. Her pillow might be firm, but the curve where his chest met his shoulder was shaped just right for her head. And…she could hear, or maybe it was just feel, the rhythm of his heartbeat. Strong and steady. She should have set up her own tent, but then she wouldn't have even begun to relax. In one way, it was torture being so close to Garrett, but his strength, the heat his big body radiated, were also comforting.

More than that, she admitted to herself that there was no one she'd rather have at her side on an operation that filled her with trepidation. He was smart, with lightning quick reactions, able to answer violence with violence in a way she'd never had to do before. And she knew, even though the two of them were done as a couple, that he'd be determined to keep her safe while also having enough respect for her skill on the job to not try to hobble her.

What more could she want?

Astonishingly, her eyelids felt heavy and her body seemed to be relaxing toward sleep.

I have to tell him, was her next-to-last thought, followed by, *Not until this is over. This isn't the right time.* They had plenty of worries without adding one so personal.

Coward, she accused herself, but didn't find an answer for that before she slid into dreams.

Chapter Eight

Cadence's eyes popped open, and she knew immediately why. Stomach roiling, she lay as still as she could. Oh, no! This was the *worst* timing.

Yeah, and what had she expected? She was at least queasy every morning, and quite often so sick to her stomach she had to run for the bathroom. This was a good reason she should have slept in her own tent.

Her head was still pillowed on Garrett's shoulder. He stirred slightly, making her realize light had filtered through the tight weave of the tent walls. Dawn was close enough, he'd be waking up any minute.

Her first movements were slow as she separated herself from him one careful inch at a time. He made a whuffing sound that might become a question. Her shaking hand found the sleeping bag zipper even as she also groped for pants and boots.

By the time she squirmed out of the sleeping bag, she was moving fast. Swallowing back the bile in her throat. Pants on, feet shoved into boots. Snatch up a roll of toilet paper. She parted the tent flap as Garrett said, "Cadence?"

"Gotta go." Run. She hated the idea of puking in the pit toilet, but what else could she do? She wouldn't want to bag her own vomit and stow it in her pack, the way she'd have to if she sprinted for the woods.

Thank God no one else was ahead of her. In fact, she didn't see any other movement around the campground. She had just enough privacy to heave, whimper and do it again. Then she wiped her mouth with a few squares of toilet paper, straightened and read her body.

Yes, she was done. She'd rinse her mouth out quick when she got back, and she knew from recent experience that she'd be fine eating breakfast. Most days, this would be it, while occasionally she had other, unpredictable bouts of nausea, but if that happened... Well, it wouldn't be hard to make an excuse to leave the trail and open enough distance from Garrett that he wouldn't be able to hear her.

Unsurprisingly, he was up, dressed in cargo pants and a T-shirt, and was firing up the stove. He looked up as she approached, though, those blue eyes sharp.

He can't know.

"You okay?" he asked.

"Sure." She shrugged. "I should have gotten up during the night, but I didn't want to. You know what that's like."

His gaze lingered on her face as if he sensed a lie, but at last he said, "Oatmeal?"

"Sure. Did you bring some, too?"

"Always have it in my pack." He rooted around in said pack, a dark green, and produced other sealed packets. "Raisins or cranberries?"

"Um...cranberries. Wait, I have some nuts, too."

She could have started rolling sleeping bags and pads, but gave herself the gift of sitting for a few minutes, watching his quick, sure movements. Once he dished up the oatmeal, he put water on to boil. He carried coffee, as did she. Unfortunately, she'd had to give up coffee for the time being. Smelling it should be okay, especially outside where any aroma dissipated fast.

When she saw the water close to boiling, she hunted for the box of tea she'd stuffed in the top of her pack and took out one bag.

"I'm in the mood for tea," she said, and handed him her mug.

That earned her another of his thoughtful and too-piercing looks, but he didn't question her. She'd read that some caffeine was all right, so she'd bought a couple different kinds of black tea. She could only imagine what he'd think if she'd produced an herbal tea!

Nobody else had stirred when she rolled up both their bags and pads while he washed their minimal dishes, dried and stowed them in his pack. He took care of the tent, since it was his, and they split up again to use the incredibly primitive facilities.

Then both donned belts with holsters and guns and swung first packs onto their backs and then rifles over their shoulder.

"You don't think they could have slipped by during the night."

"No," Garrett said. "I sleep lightly. As it was, I woke up several times when other campers got up. Somebody snored."

She wrinkled her nose as they reached the trail. "I heard that."

Gradually, they stretched their legs, slowing to use rocks to cross a stream that flowed to join the North Folk River, and plunged into heavy forest. The quiet was more profound this morning, as if even the birds were reluctant to violate it.

"Two hours ahead of us," Cadence said. "That means they could have gotten as far as Eight Stream."

"Unless they turned off."

She'd studied her map last night in minute detail. "I'm thinking Hammer Creek."

"If they can get across the river there. I kind of doubt they'd try."

Hammer Creek flowed from the higher elevation of Smith Lake and Black and White Lakes—which were officially accessible by the Flapjack Lakes trail. Climbers took that route to reach several popular climbs, including one of the park's best known: the daunting spear of rock that was Mount Cruiser. It would be logical for climbers who'd first climbed Mount Duckabush or the like farther north to look for a shortcut to Cruiser.

She could only hope Ed McCall and Alyssa Bailey had gotten an early start up that trail.

The trail was smooth; no issues with fallen branches or the mud or washouts that might have plagued it during the spring. Cadence saw a few places where understory vegetation was trampled enough to suggest someone had stepped off the trail. It was hard to tell how fresh those signs were. After the brief conversation, she and Garrett stayed silent, communicating when they paused with raised eyebrows and hand signals. She didn't really believe they would catch up so soon, but if the men were inexperienced, possibly suffering from blisters… Who knew?

"Bear," Garrett murmured, and she turned her head sharply.

A lone black bear, spattered with water, was making its way up from the river. Beady eyes fixed on them and it stopped, then lumbered across the trail right in front of them and crashed its way into the deep forest. The black bears were rarely a problem, unless a mother felt her cubs were threatened, but an occasional one became aggressive. Those who mooched food at campgrounds from people who didn't know better sometimes had to be trapped and relocated where they were less likely to encounter humans. Most often, the bears ran, just as this one had.

A squawk from her radio startled her. She pulled it from the outside pocket on her pack and adjusted the volume. Behind her, she realized Garrett was doing the same with his. She was reassured by reports from other pairs of law enforcement rangers and law enforcement officers who had started as early as she and Garrett had. Two rangers she knew well had started up the Duckabush River trail, which unfortunately began well outside the park boundaries. *At least five or six miles from a gravel or dirt forest road*, she thought. Not that the park boundary mattered, except that men on the run might see it as a trail that would lead them out of the park and onto forest roads, where they could arrange a pickup if either of their phones worked.

The best news: a helicopter was on its way from the air force base on Whidbey Island and was aiming straight for the trail that lay ahead of Garrett and Cadence.

IN THE FIRST HOURS, they heard the helicopter a few times rather than seeing it, sheltered as they were by the tall hemlock, fir and cedar forest. The pilot and a spotter reported seeing people, both hikers and climbers, but nobody meeting the right description.

Cadence and Garrett came face-to-face with one party of climbers who seemed startled to meet armed law enforcement.

When told about the manhunt, they explained that they'd spent the night at Nine Stream. "Haven't seen any foot traffic this morning at all," one of the men added, "but we did get an earlier start than a lot of people do."

They promised to stop anyone they met coming up the trail who wasn't a cop or a ranger, after which they strode out.

Watching them go, Cadence said, "The Nine Stream campground is, what, another three miles on? Are they still that far ahead of us?"

"They might have heard someone coming and just stepped off the trail. In the right place, they wouldn't have had to go more than ten feet to avoid being seen."

The lush vegetation in this river valley made that very possible.

Predictably, she argued anyway. "Or they could be somewhere else entirely."

His eyebrows climbed. "But where? In the next hours, we'll have this corner of the park blanketed by searchers. They could hunker down somewhere they won't be seen, but then what's their plan?"

"If they have enough food, they might think they can just outwait us."

"They could have done that more easily before they sped down Highway 101 in full knowledge they'd attracted pursuit," Garrett said dryly. "If they'd used their brains, they would have looked for an empty house, a garage where the Tahoe could be hidden..." He shrugged. "Now they're out of their element."

She wrinkled her nose at him. "We think."

What could he say but, "We'll find them," and hope she didn't resent what might as well be a pat on the back.

If Cadence was annoyed, it didn't show. She simply nodded and turned to continue north.

The going was slow, because they had to divert every time they spotted evidence that people had beaten a path off the trail, paths that didn't appear on the topographical map that Cadence pulled out at intervals. Most often these dwindled, or ended at an obvious wilderness campsite. Really, in this stretch the river had carved its way along the foot of steep ridges and even mountains, rising too steep above the trail to offer any easy access. Dragging a boy along, carrying borrowed packs, wearing boots that, from the description, weren't hiking or climbing boots with the needed deep-cut tread, would this pair really part from a well-trodden path to take what would be a perilous climb? Garrett couldn't see it.

Eight Stream came and went, the trail rising above the riverbank. Given the steep terrain, Garrett wasn't surprised to have to cross several avalanche slopes, covered by the usual brush and new growth. Once again, he disliked feeling so exposed, even if his uneasiness was unwarranted. The fugitives weren't going to hang around to take potshots at anyone pursuing them.

It was all he could do to get Cadence to stop to have lunch once they'd reached a sun-dappled forest. She was 100 percent focused on that kid, ready to push herself until she broke. Once he succeeded in persuading her to set her pack aside and sit on a rock on the riverbank, Garrett studied her. He wished she weren't carrying as much weight as he was. Yes, she always did when they'd hiked or climbed, but today they'd been moving faster than they would have if this outing had been recreational. She looked tired, although she'd claim he was imagining things if he said anything. After cutting ties between them, she was unlikely to appreciate any remark she saw as disparaging her capabilities. He was well aware that to this day women in law enforcement with any jurisdiction faced discrimination, and he wouldn't blame her for being prickly.

Accordingly, he made himself dig in his pack, seeing out of the corner of his eye that she was doing the same.

He also caught a glimpse of some of the contents of her pack, and realized that she'd brought medical supplies beyond the basics he always had and therefore was carrying *more* than he was.

He found a packaged nut and dried fruit mix first, even as he wondered whether he could talk her into stowing her tent under a bush to be picked up later. Or letting him carry some of those extra supplies that helped make her pack bulge.

She handed him her water bottle. He took a swig and gave it back.

"You have to hunt for lost kids on a regular basis," he observed. "They're often in as much danger as Evan is, if for different reasons."

"But that's it," she said. "It's the…the malevolence of grabbing a child, using their vulnerability."

Yeah, a child hostage raised the emotional quotient for anyone mounting an attack, but Garrett guessed that it was the ease of controlling a kid versus an adult that had motivated this particular choice. But he knew what she meant.

"You just saved a little girl," he pointed out.

"It happened so fast."

He shrugged to concede the point.

She produced some packaged cheese and crackers probably meant for school lunches, which made him smile. He enjoyed his, even if the cheese presumably wasn't the real thing.

Before she could get too antsy, he closed up his pack and said, "Ready?"

"Yes." Even after hefting her pack onto her back, she all but bounced to her feet.

Yeah, she was tougher than he'd been giving her credit for. He always found her strength surprising, given how slim she was. Self-preservation had kept him from ever saying that he thought her well-worn boots were cute in what she'd admitted was a size six.

The footbridge crossing Nine Stream was solid, leading them to the camp. He was relieved to see it empty but for two tents that had been left, any possessions zipped inside them. Cadence scribbled notes that they managed to attach to the tent flaps, informing their owners that the park was closed and they needed to proceed south to Staircase.

Then she and Garrett moved on. Shortly thereafter, the river swung to the east, while they crossed a stream and continued north. They began to gain elevation here, the trail consisting of short switchbacks. As nonrunners/hikers, he'd expect the men to founder here. Feathery hemlock trees shaded them as they ascended—and hid them from above, as it would have hidden their quarry.

The forest seemed unnaturally quiet again. Garrett was in the lead, and he realized neither of them had said anything in a while. Yeah, sure, the climb here was steep enough he felt it in his thighs and was probably breathing a little harder than he had been. He stole a look back.

Damn it, Cadence had a talent for hiding what she thought and felt that he hadn't known she possessed. He'd liked the openness of her expressions, the glow of happiness when she first saw him, the subtle displays of humor, her laughter. He'd been so sure she couldn't lie to him. Now he had to wonder if she'd been lying to him all along, and this was the real her.

Or whether she'd retreated deep inside, hiding behind a pleasant, professional facade.

She was sweating, but not breathing any harder than he was. Her head turned constantly as she searched the forest. You'd think she would stumble on the sometimes rocky trail, but she stayed sure-footed.

He glanced at his watch and discovered it was later than he had realized. They'd come on a camp pretty soon. Two Bear lacked any sanitary facilities. After that, a push to First Divide, and another camp. He guessed Cadence would expect to get that far, and even push on to a meeting with the upper Duckabush River. That's where they'd have to start making some serious decisions.

Had they been wrong in assuming these bastards weren't experienced backwoodsmen? Garrett had to wonder. Despite the various brief detours, he and Cadence had made pretty good time. They and the other pairs advancing this direction wouldn't quite come to anything resembling a hub of a wheel, but as they approached, they'd constrict the area to be searched, closing in on the threesome no matter which way they turned.

Unless, a quiet voice in the back of his head murmured, they really had holed up, maybe even watching as their pursuers strode blindly past.

Yeah, but that didn't mean they could stroll back the way they'd come. He'd followed radio traffic well enough to know the numbers of searchers continued to climb. The Tahoe had long since been towed away, and the campground should have emptied by now. With a little luck, two or three days in, there shouldn't be any vehicles left at the trailheads, either, except those left by searchers from one jurisdiction or another. Sooner or later, the men would be spotted. *Just, please, God, don't let them come face-to-face.* A shoot-out at a roadblock was one thing, standing fifty feet apart with no engine block to hide behind, another.

The designated campsite at Two Bear was laid out by a rushing creek and shaded by a thick canopy of mixed evergreen trees. *Nice*, he thought, saw it was empty and kept going.

As he and Cadence pushed on toward the pass at First Divide, following the stream, they left behind the forest for subalpine meadows filled with berry bushes and what would be a blaze of wildflowers a little later in the summer. He stopped to use his binoculars frequently.

A rustle ahead brought him to a stop. He lifted those binoculars again. He thought Cadence came close enough to walking into him that she braced a hand on his pack.

"What…?"

"Bear," he said, seeing the bushes shaking. On its own, or… No. Fifteen or twenty feet to the left, he spotted a cub. No, two—one on each side of the trail.

"Damn," he said.

"We could try to scare them."

"I don't want to face down a mama bear who thinks we've gotten too close to her cubs. It won't kill us to wait for a while."

She glared past him at the fluttering bushes heavy with ripe berries.

Garrett looked around and saw a reasonably flat rock. Cadence sighed and nodded.

He, for one, was just as glad to take off his pack for a few minutes. The back of his shirt was soaked with sweat. He sat, stretched out his legs and was able to pluck a handful of purple-blue berries.

He offered them to Cadence, who was stretching her neck and shoulders after dumping her own pack. That was as much admission as she'd ever make about the stress on her body.

"Oh, thanks, but I'm not hungry."

His body had long since forgotten their relatively scanty

lunch and was ready for a snack, at least. He shrugged and popped the berries into his mouth, the taste a burst of sweet and tart at the same time. No wonder the bear family was so happily occupied. He swiveled to pick more.

Cadence did take out her water bottle, drank from it and offered it to him. He did the same and handed it back, grimacing at the purple stain on his fingers.

"What if they don't move on?"

"You know they will sooner or later. I'd say I'm sorry our targets didn't stumble over mama bear, except I'm guessing they'd have shot her."

"Yeah, most people don't realize a bullet or two won't stop a full-grown bear, but given the kind of armaments they're probably carrying..."

They might well have killed the mother bear, orphaning two cubs too young to survive on their own.

"Are you planning to stay around for a while?" she asked, her tone casual, something not as casual beneath.

Stay around *here*?

He flicked a glance at her. *Oh.* She meant on the Olympic peninsula, working his current job. She was staring straight ahead, as she'd been prone to do yesterday and today. God forbid she meet his eyes.

"I'm not setting a date to go," he said after a minute. Feeling his forehead crease, he thought again that maybe he should, now that Cadence and he weren't seeing each other. But he continued, "Living with someone can be difficult when you're not used to it, but...it's been good getting to know my grandfather."

At last, her head turned and she had a recognizable expression on her face: startlement. "What do you mean, *getting to know*?"

Why had he told her that? There was a reason he just didn't talk about family. He rolled his suddenly tight shoulders.

"I didn't know my grandparents when I was a kid," he said, voice clipped. Something he didn't understand compelled him to continue. "I didn't even know I had them. My mother—" wow, those two words felt strange in his mouth "—hated them. She was, uh, pretty disturbed. She never talked about being a kid."

"Did she…run away or something?"

"Yeah, when she was fifteen or sixteen, I think."

"Do you know what was going on?"

Why had he opened his damn mouth? But now that he had, he reluctantly said, "No. She was…classic. I used to think she was screwed up by an abusive childhood." He jerked one shoulder. "I guess she did butt heads with my grandmother, but Grandma… What can I say? She was a good woman. She…really broke down when I showed up on their doorstep." He'd grieved her death from cancer only a couple of years after he located them. Shaking that off, he said, "Looking back, I think my mother had to be mentally ill. If doctors ever prescribed pills, she didn't stay on them. Fortunately, except for the early years, she only appeared in my life once in a great while."

"Oh, Garrett." Cadence's voice was as soft as a touch. He'd rather have had the touch, except he couldn't let himself be that vulnerable.

He shrugged. "Long time ago."

"Is she dead?" she asked hesitantly.

His jaw clenched, and he had to let a minute pass before he was able to speak without emotion. "Once I became a cop, I checked. She OD'd…four or five years before that. So fifteen years or more ago. Can't even picture her face." Which was a lie.

This time, she laid her hand on his bare forearm. He looked down, feeling a lurch at the sight of her long, graceful fingers and fine-boned hand and wrist. All he could do was clench his teeth and wait until she withdrew it.

Neither said another word until the rustles just north of them subsided, and he hefted his pack onto his back and rose. "Probably safe to go on."

He was grateful that Cadence followed suit without remark.

Chapter Nine

"I haven't heard the helicopter in a while," Cadence said, as soon as the realization crossed her mind.

"They're losing the light and need to get on the ground. They promise to be back come morning."

Oh, wonderful. She should have paid more attention to radio traffic, but the steep ascent to First Divide, a high ridge that offered a sweeping view of the mountains rearing to each side, had a monotony despite the views that allowed her brain to sink into a form of apathy. Wow, she didn't like to think how unobservant she'd been!

Really, what thinking she'd done had to do with the man who was a mostly silent presence behind her. She was bothered to have to keep reminding herself that there was nothing personal between her and Garrett anymore. She winced. Well, except for the baby he didn't know about yet.

So why had he told her about his mother and at least sketched in the childhood that explained so much about him? Oh, maybe he'd had a kind, steady father, but she would bet anything that wasn't the case. Commitment to a woman might truly be beyond his imagining if he'd spent his life in foster care or group homes. A lifetime of temporary relationships. Did the fact that he'd told her as much as he did, and so out of the blue, suggest he was showing a willingness to open up to her?

Right. All she had to do was remember the expression on his face when she'd asked if he had any interest in the possibility that their relationship could become more. Shock, followed by an implacable mask.

Yeah, no.

She forced her thoughts to focus on the here and now. They'd almost have to stop at the designated campsite at First Divide. Or… For the first time, she noticed how quickly the sky was dimming. She had a faint memory of climbing Mount Hopper with a fellow ranger when she first started at the park. A faint but obvious trail turned off just before First Divide. She vaguely remembered it opening eventually into a beautiful alpine meadow that lay at the foot of a steep boulder field.

"You okay?" Garrett asked from behind her.

She must have slowed down. "Yes, but I remembered that access to Mount Hopper should be coming up on the right anytime. It wouldn't make *sense* for them to go that way, but…"

"Nothing they're doing makes sense," he growled. "Especially if they have binoculars, they could have caught sight of us coming up behind them and wanted to get out of sight."

"We almost have to look," she said, without enthusiasm. One more wasted detour.

"Anyplace we could set up camp?" Garrett asked.

"It's only a few hundred yards before Home Sweet Home." Personally, she thought the name of the designated campsite atop First Divide was nauseatingly sweet, but it did have restroom facilities of a sort. "We can sleep there and turn back in the morning. Unless the helicopter gets here in time to do a sweep of that track and the side of the mountain."

"Makes sense," he agreed, without commenting on her wishful thinking.

Lord, she hoped the campground was empty...except being utterly alone with Garrett would increase her tension. And decrease the chance she could avoid notice if she woke up with her usual morning upset stomach.

When they arrived, the meadow was entirely empty.

"Pick your spot," Garrett said wryly, looking around.

She wanted to say, *You set up your tent over there, and I'll put up mine on the exact opposite side of the meadow.* Unfortunately, she had too much pride to give away any hurt feelings.

"Let's make it by that clump of trees," she suggested. "Not quite so...open."

Her chosen spot wasn't far from the toilet, either, just in case. Or the trees would give her another option.

"Works for me."

Once they'd dropped their packs and begun unfastening straps, she said casually, "I might set up my own tent tonight. There's plenty of room."

He stopped what he was doing to scowl at her. "I make you that uncomfortable?"

She hated seeing how still he held himself. "It's not that," she said weakly.

"Then what?"

"You wouldn't like more room to stretch out?"

"No." His jaws worked. "I want to be able to see you. I don't like the idea someone could sneak up, slit the tent and grab you without me having any idea what was happening."

Her body might have given a betraying jerk. Damn. Now,

if she insisted, she wouldn't be able to sleep a wink. *Thank you, Garrett.*

"You win," she conceded.

"I'm not trying to—" He hesitated.

Given the awkwardness, Cadence didn't look at him. "No, you're right. It could work the opposite way, too. You could be killed without me even knowing."

He still hadn't moved. "It won't happen. I just… Call me paranoid."

She made a face. "No, it's okay. You're right. I'll sleep better."

After a moment, he nodded and went back to spreading a tarp on the ground and setting up his tent.

Given her aching back and shoulders, she kind of wished she'd left hers behind. It just hadn't occurred to her… No, the surprise had been his insistence on pairing with her. He'd made it next to impossible for her to say, *No, that's not happening.*

And how would she feel if she had rearranged the pairings? Behind Garrett's back, Cadence grimaced. She wouldn't have trusted any of the other deputies the way she did Garrett. She would have thought about him, worried he and his partner might be the ones to come unexpectedly on their quarry. If he'd been gunned down…

Had she really convinced herself she wasn't in love with him anymore? Like that happened practically overnight. He'd hurt her, she *needed* to move past these feelings, but she hadn't yet. And wouldn't be able to until this was over, she'd told him about her pregnancy and they'd parted ways. It might be best if he did go back to Seattle, she thought. *Out of sight, out of mind.*

Or so she wanted to believe.

Maybe *she* should start looking into a transfer. Except

she didn't have a clue what kind of future she'd have in the park service. And…what if Garrett wanted some contact with his child?

CADENCE HAD FALLEN quiet after they settled whether they'd share a tent or not.

They parted to use the facilities and briefly discussed which of their limited menu options they'd have for dinner. Garrett had gotten on the radio and identified their location and plan for morning, listening as other teams did the same.

The pair assigned to the Duckabush River trail had made good time, but after starting out a day later than Garrett and Cadence, were overnighting at the Ten Mile encampment on One Too Many Creek.

Too many what? Garrett wondered, but didn't linger on the question.

Jefferson County deputies Ed McCall and Alyssa Bailey had explored every trail, any hint of a spur leaving it, and nook and cranny of the cluster of lakes they'd been assigned to investigate. They'd scrambled to Smith Lake, the headwaters for Hammer Creek, and finally backtracked to set off behind Garrett and Cadence. They were likely too far behind to be helpful, but Garrett had stayed uneasily conscious all day that their quarry could have hidden and now be hustling down the trail and thinking they were home free.

Ian Sutherland and Tyler Murray had reached Sundown Lake, and since there'd been sightings of the men and boy so far north, were to be picked up by the helicopter in the morning and set down on the Quinault River Trail, potentially to connect with a pair of rangers who were already in the Enchanted Valley, a favorite destination of backpackers that lay along the Quinault River. A pair of deputies from

Clallam County were heading southwest along the west fork of the Dosewallips River.

All well and good, but too few of them were spread over a vast stretch of the national park, separated by sharp-toothed mountain peaks, rivers, long ridges and in places, dense forests.

Brooding as he ate the meal Cadence had prepared, he said finally, "We need another helicopter."

"Yeah. I wonder if there's been a crisis elsewhere?"

He grunted. "You'd think they'd tell us. Having to close so much of the park with the height of summer coming up so soon can't be good for the National Park Service image."

She made a face. "I can only imagine the press. I mean, there have been other manhunts in the park, but none that started with dynamite, a cop being shot and killed, a dangerous pursuit on Highway 101 and the abduction of a child from a campground."

"Never mind the heads they bashed at said campground." He paused. "And the number of witnesses who are no doubt eagerly talking to reporters."

"The head ranger must be having conniptions."

He laughed. "Maybe we should count our blessings. Here we are, alone in beautiful country, stars coming out overhead…"

"And having no idea how close those killers are."

Mildly chagrined, he said, "You're right."

"But you are, too. It *is* a beautiful night." She sounded faintly surprised.

Romantic, even. With an intensity that shook him, Garrett wished nothing had changed. That despite the seriousness of their purpose, they would make love once they bedded down for the night.

His body responded to the mere thought, leaving him

grateful for the darkness. No fires were allowed in the backcountry, which encouraged early to bed, early to rise. Which was fine, but days were long in the Pacific Northwest at this time of year. Fortunately, not quite as long, given the mountains rising to the west of them, especially Mount Olympus. The sun dropped below those considerably sooner than when it painted magnificent colors over the curve of the earth seen when you sat on a bluff above the Pacific Ocean.

He knew that, because he and Cadence had rented a cabin for a couple of nights at Kalaloch Resort on the ocean. Holding hands, they'd walked on the beach, rolling up their pants and letting the foam from waves wash over their feet despite brisk spring temperatures. He remembered seagulls crying, piles of driftwood at the foot of the bluff. Those had been a couple of the best days of his life.

Tension gripped him. In response, he rolled his shoulders. It had been a good place to take a woman, that's all. Once he started up something with someone else— His mind hit a wall.

What was wrong with him?

"I'm ready to go to sleep," Cadence said, reaching into her pack. "At least, I'm ready to try."

"You're right. The sooner the better, so we can be up at first light again."

They shared the cool water in a pan to brush their teeth, then parted ways briefly before returning to the tent. He let her crawl in first and gave her a few minutes to strip down before he knelt and followed. Not like he could have seen her, but he didn't have the right anymore to savor the sound of her squirming to get a shirt over her head, or pants down those long legs.

When he thought about it, she'd either moved really fast,

or had remained partially dressed. Yeah, he'd do that, too, he decided. Just in case they heard something, he wanted to be ready to go. He laid his rifle to one side, but set his handgun within easy reach as he had last night and suspected she'd done the same.

Then he balled a fleece quarter-zip to serve as a pillow and stretched out on his back, very aware that she lay curled away from him, her knees and face all but pressed against the tent wall.

"Good night."

"Sleep tight," she murmured, just as she had on other occasions when they'd been together.

The ensuing silence wasn't an easy one. He was willing to bet she regretted reminding him in any way of their time together.

And, damn, he couldn't imagine dropping peacefully off to sleep at any time in the foreseeable future. Reaching for her as he had last night… She couldn't have made her wishes clearer.

Brooding held sleep off long enough to make him tense with the knowledge he'd be tired tomorrow. He must have finally dropped off, though, because he surfaced to find that he and Cadence were plastered together, her back to his front, and he'd taken his arm out of the sleeping bag so he could wrap it around her. His hand had found its way to her breast. Still half-asleep, he gently squeezed her breast and rubbed his palm over her nipple, already firm and ripe. For just a moment, he'd have sworn her back arched to push her breast more fully into his hand, but when he went still and held his breath, nothing happened. Temptation tore at him, but if he coaxed her, half-asleep, into making love with him, she'd regret it in the morning. He'd hate that. What's more, it wouldn't help his cause with her. Whether she really was asleep or only pretending, he couldn't violate her decision.

He forced himself to release her and pull his arm back into his own sleeping bag.

CADENCE'S FIRST THOUGHT on waking was that she wanted to roll over and go back to sleep. Despite her exhaustion, she hadn't slept well. There'd been an interlude she might have dreamed when Garrett was touching her the way she loved. What's more, her right hip ached and—

Her second full awareness was powerful: she needed to upchuck, and she needed to do it *now*.

On an involuntary moan, she scrambled out of her sleeping bag, pushed aside the tent flap and lurched out onto her hands and knees. Her stomach was already heaving. Oh, God, oh God, she had to get away.

But she knew too well that Garrett had reared up and gotten far enough forward for his head and shoulders to poke from the tent.

"Cadence?"

She tried to speak but made a retching sound. She crawled away but was too sick to rise to her feet. Suddenly, an aluminum pan appeared in front of her and she gave up, snatching it from Garrett's hands and puking. *Please let it be big enough*, she begged. *Don't let me make this even worse than it already is.*

A big hand smoothed hair from her face. He was crouching beside her, she realized. When she was finally done and started to sag, he supported her until she managed to get into a sitting position, albeit swaying.

She couldn't look at him. Despite the gentleness of his hands, he hadn't said a word, not even a soothing, *You'll be fine.*

He set the pan out of her sight and magically produced a water bottle. She rinsed, spat into another dish and did it again. Gradually, her muscles unwound. This nausea had hit harder than usual.

Of course it had, given that this was the worst of all possible times.

"Better?" His first word was almost kind, if she couldn't hear an undertone.

"I think so," she mumbled. "Wow."

"Yeah. Wow."

"I need to—" She gestured vaguely.

"You need to talk to me," he said in a hard voice. "You were sick yesterday morning, too, weren't you?"

She could lie, but would he believe her? And...even if this timing sucked, she had to tell him sooner or later. It looked like it would be sooner.

She bobbed her head.

He cursed. "Were you ever going to tell me?"

For the first time, she let herself look up, seeing anger in his eyes and thinning his mouth. "Of course I was." Feeling like a rag that had just been wrung out, she couldn't summon any vehemence. "This—" she waved a hand "just all blew up so suddenly. I wasn't ready."

Garrett swore again. "Did it ever occur to you that you had no business throwing an overloaded pack on your back and storming off into the wilderness after a pair of killers *when you're pregnant*?"

"No. This is my job! Women don't sit around twiddling their thumbs because they're pregnant! I'm *fine*—"

"Except for needing to puke your guts out on a regular basis?" He was furious, and not hiding it.

"It's mostly mornings. Not that big a deal. Now, if you'll let me brush my teeth, we should get ready."

His "Not a chance," was soft and ominous. "This makes me wonder if you ever would have told me. How long have you known you were pregnant?"

"Does it matter? I'm not very far along." Six weeks? No. "Maybe two months now. Women often miscarry in the first three months. That's why it's common not to share the news so early."

"With their partners?"

"We're not partners!" she flared, pain mixing with white-hot anger. Her stomach lurched again.

"You're denying I'm the father?"

"Of course I'm not!"

"Then we're partners whether you like it or not."

Oh, that made her mad and stiffened her spine. Glaring at him, she snapped, "You've made plain how uninterested you are in any ties at all! I would have told you, and if you want to be involved in the baby's life—"

His stare blistered her. "You thought I *wouldn't* be?"

"I…" Cadence closed her eyes. "Can we dial this back? I feel lousy. I'd like to clean up and get dressed."

Muscles knotted in his stubbled jaw. "Yeah," he said tightly. "Go ahead."

Radiating tension, he turned his back on her and reached inside the tent for clothes, dragging his pack out. "Go ahead," he said shortly, nodding at the tent.

More than getting dressed, what she really wanted was to scrub her mouth out and have something to eat or drink that would improve the taste and settle any lingering queasiness, but it did make sense to put on some clothes first. It was a way of armoring herself, and she'd feel a little less pathetic.

In the dimness of the tent, she contorted to pull up her pants before digging a clean bra and shirt out of her pack. Socks, boots. And she could only imagine how awful her hair was. She took the time to brush it smooth and braid it as she did most mornings.

She composed herself.

He'd calm down. Garrett wasn't an unreasonable man. He'd been the one to lay out his terms, the one to close any door to altering those terms. The pregnancy had taken her by surprise as much as it had him. They'd used birth control without fail. Usually, two versions, since he had always insisted on donning a condom even though she'd worn a patch. Which, yes, had gone missing a while ago, but she hadn't worried because of the condoms.

No method of birth control was 100 percent, condoms least of all.

What she didn't dare tell him was that, however unexpected and unplanned this pregnancy was, shock hadn't been her only emotion when that test had come up positive. She wanted this baby.

And if he knew that, he'd accuse her of getting pregnant on purpose, which would sour any possibility of civility going forward.

She was having this baby, whether he liked it or not.

Chapter Ten

Squatting on an upended log, Garrett bent over the stove. Water in the pan boiled by the time Cadence crawled out of the tent. "Coffee?" he asked. "Or tea?"

"Tea, please. I'll get it out of my pack." She disappeared again briefly, dragging her pack when she reappeared. A moment later she handed over a tea bag.

He was trying to stomp down on the anger, but all that did was make him aware of how much else he felt. Too much, a lot of it unfamiliar. His chest was about to explode from the pressure.

Expecting his hands to be shaking, he was surprised by their steadiness when he poured the hot water into the two cups and set the pan back down. He'd need to refill it to heat water for their oatmeal, but that could wait. Garrett just wished he knew what to say.

No, he knew the first thing he had to ask.

"You planning to have this baby?"

Her head shot up. "Yes!"

"Pregnancy will torpedo your career."

Outrage remaining on her fine-boned face, she opened her mouth…then closed it. "I've…been putting off finding out what park service policy is."

He clenched his teeth, the better to keep his mouth shut.

Cadence bent her head and gazed into the steeping tea as if it could offer her a prophecy. "I know I'll have to take time off," she said softly. "Maybe...try to get shifted from the law enforcement focus."

He had to say this. "We need to get married."

"What?" She lifted her head to stare at him. "Don't be ridiculous! This isn't the fifties!"

"It's still the right thing to do. I can get you and the baby on my health insurance, take care of you when you can't work."

"If I can't keep working, I'll go home."

He'd been afraid she would say that. He needed her here, where he could see her daily, with much the same intensity as he'd needed to share a tent with her.

"That's my baby," he ground out.

Hot color blazed on her cheeks. "No, it's *my* baby."

His gaze lowered from her face, and when she looked down she blinked at the sight of her hand splayed over her abdomen in instinctive protection.

He took a deep breath and let it out. "Ours."

Their eyes met.

"Why are you so worked up?" She sounded genuinely puzzled. "You were really blunt when you told me this isn't anything you want. Marriage, children... Maybe you just weren't interested in anything lasting with me, but you will be eventually with someone else."

There wouldn't be anybody else.

"I don't know," she went on. "But... It doesn't matter. I'm not trying to trap you into this, if that's what you're thinking. If you'll pay child support, I'll be grateful, but I won't even hold you to that. I can cope."

He felt sick with the knowledge that this was what she thought of him, that he was a man who could shrug off the knowledge he had a kid out there somewhere, not willing to make any effort to stay in contact or pay his share of expenses.

Countering her perception meant baring himself in ways he never had before, but he didn't see a choice. "I...don't know who my father is. Whether he knew my mother was pregnant or not. From what I remember about her...he was unlikely to be any prize." His throat tried to close. He pushed past it, voice hoarse. "I will never allow any child of mine to grow up feeling unwanted."

Seeing her expression soften, Garrett had to look away. He hated pity.

"I...won't try to keep you from being a father," Cadence said softly. "I promise."

"Then marry me."

She shook her head. "No. I won't marry a man who doesn't love *me*. First and foremost. That's...a recipe for disaster." Her mouth twisted. "I should say, for a quick divorce. You *know* that's not what you want."

"You're wrong. I want us to raise this child together. All of us living in the same house." This certainty was only one of the tangled feelings he hardly understood.

Her head shook again, hard enough that her braid flopped over her shoulder. "That's what your grandfather would have said in this situation. People have children out of wedlock all the time these days. We can share custody without the bitterness and anger that an eventual divorce would brew. Wouldn't that be better?"

"No." He let her see and hear that he wouldn't change his mind. "You said yourself, we were good together. We have what it takes to..." He stumbled over how to finish the sentence. Be happy together? For a lifetime? Something he'd never imagined being possible, but Cadence had shaken some of his preconceptions, he couldn't deny that. Why else had he been so stunned when she'd shrugged and said *See you around*?

"I saw the expression on your face that day in the café," she said quietly. "You're not in love with me, or even close. You were shocked that I'd imagine for a minute that our relationship might be going anywhere besides bed when we can both get off work at the same time. Say what you will, but you were clear from the beginning."

"This is why you confronted me, isn't it?" The realization had just jumped into his head. "You already knew you were pregnant."

"No." She hesitated. "I guess I'd begun to suspect. And… before I found out, I did need to know how you felt about me, whether you'd changed your mind about the future."

"If you'd explained—"

Her dark eyes sparked with anger. "You're not hearing me. I needed the truth. And no, I won't marry you because of the baby."

He opened his mouth without any idea what he was going to say, but she shook him off.

"Garrett, we have more important things to do right now. There's a scared boy out there depending on us. I'm not having the baby tomorrow. Even assuming all goes well, we have seven months to talk about how we'll handle things in the future. Okay?"

No, it wasn't okay. Garrett wanted everything nailed down. Too much of his life had been a walk along the sharp edge of a knife blade. A teeter, and he'd go down. It had happened too often. But she was right to remind him of priorities. Her refusal to even consider marrying him was so adamant, it was clear he wasn't going to crack it in the immediate future.

"Have you seen a doctor?"

"No. I…did two separate pregnancy tests, and they were both positive. That's all I know right now."

God. How was he supposed to throw on his pack and march up the trail hunting killers, when his backup was a woman carrying his baby? When he knew that, if things blew up on them, he was at risk of losing both of them?

The baby was a few cells, he told himself. A fantasy. And he wasn't in love with Cadence—she was right about that. He felt more than he had let himself admit, but love? No. He felt…responsible, sure, but he had to stop himself from getting carried away.

So he forced himself to give a clipped nod and said, "I'll make the oatmeal if you want to roll up our sleeping bags."

Her eyes lingered on him, but he didn't let himself try to read anything in them. She said, "Sure," nothing special in her agreement.

They ate in complete silence. Afterward, he took down the tent and stuffed it in its bag, rolled the tarp with his pad and stowed everything back in his pack. He looked around, seeing that Cadence was doing the same. A few dusty prints, some flattened grass, was all they'd leave behind. That seemed wrong, given how momentous the past hour had been.

CADENCE STUMBLED TWICE in the first five minutes because she wasn't paying attention to where she was putting her feet. She had to hope he was being more observant in other ways than she could claim to be, too.

They quickly retraced their way to the spur trail she might not have noticed had she not been looking for it yesterday—and if she hadn't been here before, last summer. The trail curved around a slope, and she could faintly hear the stream that they would encounter ahead. There was still enough snowmelt, it must be running higher than it would later in the summer.

They reached the meadow, as pretty as she'd remembered it. Steep boulder field and stark rock of the mountain. She looked up toward the summit.

Garrett startled her when he spoke. "They wouldn't want to climb a mountain."

"Unless they thought that trail goes somewhere else?"

He cocked a brow.

"You're right. They wouldn't be able to hide above the tree line, and they must have heard the helicopter yesterday and guessed it'll be back today."

"I agree. Let's get back to First Divide."

Fortunately, they hadn't lost more than half an hour, if that. Garrett strode in the lead, his long legs making the pace effortless for him. She didn't quite have to jog, but close. Truly, she didn't mind; she shared his sense of urgency.

They passed the still-empty campsite they'd left so recently without slowing and almost immediately began the descent. And, ugh. Downhill was harder on the legs than uphill. She didn't usually notice, but after sleeping so poorly last night—

Garrett stopped suddenly, frowning. "Do you hear—?"

The crack of a gunshot made her jerk and spin around. Was someone shooting at *them*?

As if she'd spoken aloud, Garrett said tersely, "Too far away." He edged past her and broke into a bounding run down the trail. Thinking she heard shouts, she did the same, seeing he'd already pulled the Glock he carried on his hip. She groped for the snap on her holster and managed to get her hand on the butt of her gun without tripping and face-planting.

Crack.

Another shot. Handgun, she thought. A bellow. Thuds that made her think someone was running away? Climbing toward them, or dropping downslope?

She was mostly looking at Garrett's back, and what glimpses she had ahead were limited by bends in the trail and forest.

Abruptly he slowed, as if somehow he'd been able to pinpoint how far away those gunshots had been. She didn't like the prickling feeling that a watcher could be hiding among the trees.

Garrett signaled for her to stop and remain silent with a flattened hand, then eased forward. Now he gripped his pistol in a two-handed firing position. Cadence hastily imitated him. She was a heck of a shot at the range, but had so little experience actually firing it in action.

She'd fired when she had to a couple of weeks ago. The reminder gave her confidence. Still, goose bumps pricked her skin and she listened with everything in her.

The trail dropped sharply, a switchback turn ahead keeping them from seeing anything beyond it. Garrett moved carefully, tension in every line of his body.

A moan drifted to them, the only sound she could hear. Even birds had gone silent.

Ahead of her, Garrett said suddenly, "Oh, hell." He didn't relax his stance, but he moved faster. She couldn't see past him… Then she did.

Two people sprawled across the trail, their body positions so *wrong* that it took her a moment to realize why. One lay ominously still, the other whimpered and tried to push himself up. He failed, groaned and then managed to turn his head. He'd seen Garrett, she realized.

The injured were both men, she saw. The eleven-year-old boy hadn't been dropped here like a discarded rag doll.

Garrett rushed to the two, looked down, then paused and glanced back at her. He took one hand from his weapon long enough to point ahead, waited for her nod and kept going.

With complete irrationality, she wanted to beg him not to risk himself advancing close behind men who'd just gunned down two more victims.

It was immediately obvious that the bulk of the packs explained in part why these men's sprawl was so awkward. The moaning guy had been able to roll to his side, but the second man, unconscious or dead, lay bowed backward over his, the position painful to see.

The coils of rope strapped to their packs told her these were climbers.

Cadence blocked her fear from her mind, set down her pack and laid her own gun down where she could grab it quickly. Then she knelt beside the conscious man. "You were shot."

"Yeah," he pushed out between gritted teeth. "What the—?"

"You must not have gotten word that the park is closed."

She doubted he'd taken in what she said. Blood soaked his pant leg. He clutched that leg in agony. Cadence pulled his pack off his shoulders and set it down so that she could use it to elevate his leg. If the bullet had opened an artery... She tore open her pack and took out gauze pads, ripping the packaging, pressing several against his thigh even as she scanned his body for other wounds without seeing any.

Sweat dripped from his face, and his eyes were wild. "Not me. Take care of Jeff."

"Can you hold this?"

He nodded with difficulty and pushed himself up on

one elbow. When she placed his hand over the thick pad, his tendons strained on the back of his hand. Even then, she paused for an instant, watching to see how fast blood soaked those pads.

Not as much as she'd feared.

A part of her didn't forget for a second that Garrett was putting himself out there, and alone. But she was where she needed to be.

Accordingly, she swiveled on her knees to examine the man she'd suspected was dead from first sight. Seeing glazed eyes fixed on the sky and utter stillness, she knew she'd been right. Nonetheless, she quickly checked for a pulse in his throat and felt nothing. She yanked up his shirt and took a look at the obvious bullet wound in his immobile chest. There wasn't very much blood. It was the living who gushed blood, not the dead. The force had driven him backward. She thought the bullet had gone through his heart, and he'd been dead in an instant. Certainly before he hit the ground.

A part of her wanted to move him so that he didn't look so horribly uncomfortable, but she couldn't. Investigators would photograph and examine this scene. She'd do enough damage saving one life. She had no excuse for rearranging this man.

From behind her came a gasped, "Is he—?"

She struggled to compose her face before she swiveled again. "I'm sorry. There's nothing I can do."

His eyes squeezed shut. "God."

GARRETT DIDN'T DARE move as fast as he'd have liked. This was like clearing a building. Slow and careful. As cool as the early morning was, sweat stung his eyes. In the back of his mind, he couldn't help thinking how close by these bastards had been last night. Not so close they'd heard him and Cadence talking, or they'd be dead, but why hadn't he gone on enough to be sure they were truly alone?

A flash of red caught his eye. Was that the boy? The men wore black. Backpacks…green and navy blue. If the boy lagged behind…would a few carefully placed shots give him a chance to run?

They couldn't be moving fast, or he'd surely hear them, Garrett thought. Had they caught a glimpse of him? If so, were they lying in wait?

A crackly voice came from his radio and he winced, freeing a hand to turn down the volume. A branch cracked ahead, followed by a muttered curse. Was there any chance they'd understand that they were screwed, that escape was no longer possible?

Sure, that's why they'd just shot two unarmed mountain climbers who were no real threat to them. Men who likely wouldn't even have been able to report the encounter until they had cell phone service two days from now.

Garrett's foot slid a little on a slanted face of a boulder that formed part of the descent. He regained his balance quickly. Eased toward the next bend in the trail. And, hell, didn't see in time a loose rock that tumbled away from his booted foot.

Gunfire erupted. He felt a hard punch in his chest as he flung himself to one side. Bullets ripped shreds from the bark of trees all around him and pinged off rock. He hit the ground hard and rolled until he slammed to a stop against one of those trees. Damn, his arm stung and he wondered if he'd just broken a few ribs. He managed to get his Glock out in firing position and yelled, "Police! Put those guns down! We have your Tahoe and the weapons, and we know who you are!" *He* didn't, but someone would by now. "You have nowhere to go!"

At the next barrage of shots, he scrambled farther from the trail and pressed his back to the largest tree he saw. They weren't even bothering to aim, just spraying bullets everywhere. Thank god Cadence hadn't come with him. He'd give a lot to return fire…but without an adequate sightline, the risk of killing the boy was too high.

Of course, that's why those two slugs had snatched him.

When quiet descended, Garrett pushed himself to his knees, and risked stealing a look around the rough-barked tree trunk blocking his body. He saw absolutely nothing except fresh wood chips and small, feathery branches on the ground. He heard something, though: a snarled voice that came to him so faintly he knew they were running again.

He let loose of some language he rarely used, and let his head fall back and bump the tree trunk. He wouldn't accomplish anything continuing the pursuit right now. At least he knew exactly where his quarry was, if not which direction they'd choose when they reached the intersection with the Duckabush trail, not much over a mile ahead. But others were closing in. Garrett would feel more confident, if not for the boy meant to be their shield.

Chapter Eleven

Cadence heard Garrett before she saw him. Of course he'd know she was guarding her patient in case Garrett was dead and the gunmen had turned around, thinking they could retrace their steps to escape.

"It's me," he called, and she whimpered in relief. She'd never been so scared in her life as she had been when she heard that fuselage of gunshots. At that instant, she'd been acutely aware that she loved him, whether she wanted to or not. No matter what, he was the father of the baby she carried. Thinking he'd been killed...

Hands shaking now, she lowered her gun.

Maybe because she was already rattled, she was instantly aware that he looked different. A livid scratch crossed his cheek. And...that was blood on his upper arm. Mostly, though, it was his eyes. His usual calm was nowhere to be seen. Instead, she saw a wildness that might be desperation.

"You're hurt."

"Nothing serious." Not even blinking, he crossed the distance separating them before he once lowered his gaze to take in the injured man—and the dead one. "Help on its way?"

"Yes, the helicopter shouldn't be more than fifteen minutes out. Ryan needs a hospital." She swallowed. "His friend is dead."

"Yeah." He'd pulled gruff sympathy from somewhere. He nodded at the man she'd doctored to the best of her ability, but who she suspected would need surgery. No exit wound, so somebody would have to extract the bullet as well as patching up the damage.

Garrett lowered his pack to the ground beside her and crouched to meet Ryan's eyes. "I'm sorry we didn't have any way to issue a general warning to people who weren't carrying a SAT radio."

Ryan Lavosky still lay flat on the ground, his leg elevated, but he'd mastered the pain well enough to talk. "We were climbing," he said in a near monotone. "Mount Duckabush first, then O'Neil Peak. Thought about doing Mount Hopper, but our supplies were running low." He grimaced. "We didn't get that far, anyway, as it turned out."

Garrett rested a hand on the injured man's shoulder and squeezed lightly. "I imagine Cadence has told you what triggered the manhunt."

"Yeah." He seemed to take a minute just to breathe before he said, "I don't know if they'd have let us by, but Jeff—my friend." Seeing Garrett's nod, Ryan said, "He's a cop." His flinch was obvious. "I mean, was. Ah, King County Sheriff's Department. He started to give them hell for carrying guns in the park, and then he asked that boy if he was all right."

A nerve jerked beneath Garrett's eye.

"If he'd just kept his mouth shut—"

"They might have let you by," Garrett said. "But they just as well might not have. They're volatile, and incredibly violent. No hesitation, as you saw."

Tears glazed the guy's eyes, but he blinked them away. "You're bleeding," he said, noticing Garrett's arm.

"Just grazed."

Cadence said, "Let me see it."

He didn't argue, and she found he was right. Which didn't mean he didn't hurt. The groove was deep enough to guarantee a scar. Trying to hide how bothered she was to see him injured, she cleaned up the ugly gash and bandaged it. When she was done, he lifted his arm and rotated it a few times before seeming satisfied.

In the meantime, she'd been inspecting him. Her gaze settled in horror on a tear—or was it a hole?—in his shirt. Right smack in the middle of his chest.

Fingering it, she said, "What's this?" Her voice came out a little bit too high.

"You know I'm wearing my vest."

She wore hers, too, but—Oh, god. "A few inches lower, and that wouldn't have helped."

He grimaced. "Now, *that* hurts like a—" He cut off what he'd been about to say. "I might have cracked my sternum. Or ribs."

Cadence sank back on her heels. *"Might?"*

"I've been shot a couple of times before. The vest probably saved my life. Some pain for a month or so, that's nothing."

If she wasn't mistaken, he was admitting to having taken bullets at least three times, counting today. He'd talked some about his years with Seattle PD, but being shot hadn't been included in any of those stories.

Her teeth wanted to chatter, but she wouldn't let them. "I have cold packs."

"I'm…not real comfortable taking off the vest while we're exposed like this."

Her head turned sharply toward the trail behind him. "You think—?"

"No, I don't." He caught her hand in his. "But we can't rule anything out."

"No." Foolishly, she had ceased being watchful the minute she heard his voice.

"Company coming," Garrett said, and she realized she'd been hearing the helicopter for a few minutes. "It won't be able to land here. We may need to carry Ryan up to First Divide."

As it turned out, the hovering monster above them lowered a Stokes basket, essentially a backboard in a cage, and they strapped Ryan in.

He held out a hand and mouthed the words, "Thank you."

Cadence had been thinking earlier while she waited for Garrett, and now, once the injured man had been lifted on high and disappeared into the open door of the helicopter, she used the radio to request they take the friend's body, too.

Garrett seemed to understand that the pilot or medic would be answering to orders from the park ranger. He used the delay to take detailed photos of the body with his phone. Cadence hadn't wanted to do that earlier—it might have seemed sort of cold-blooded to Ryan—but Garrett was using his head.

Eventually permission came in. Leaving the body of a visitor to the park where it might be dragged away and dismembered by bears or other wildlife wasn't a good option, but neither would be asking Cadence and Garrett to stay put for what might be hours to protect the remains. Eventually the body—Jeff Yonker—was also lifted to disappear into the helicopter, both men's packs accompanying him.

The helicopter pilot told her that their intention was to fly low and look for the men and boy before taking Ryan to the hospital.

"Should be back in a couple of hours," he said. "Faster if we can connect with an ambulance."

Probably she should have told somebody about Garrett's injuries, but she'd left that decision to him. If he thought he could go on, that was his business.

And when they were so close behind...

Now THAT THE adrenaline had ebbed, Garrett felt worse than he had admitted to Cadence. That didn't mean he needed to be hauled off to the hospital. Not like doctors could do a thing for cracked or broken ribs or breastbone except for wrapping them, and he could have her do that later if necessary.

Neither of them moved as the roar of the helicopter gradually diminished. Finally, he said, "This isn't a great place to stop."

"Are you sure you're okay to go on?"

"Yeah. We won't be catching up in the near future, though, and I wouldn't mind a chance to sit along the way for a few minutes."

"Did you, um—" she pressed her lips together "—well, shoot back?"

"No." Damn, he wanted to wrap her in his arms, both to soothe the anxiety on her face and because holding her would comfort him. Her stiff posture suggested she wouldn't be receptive, however. So he nodded at their packs. "Let's clean up and get moving until we find a good place to stop. We can talk while we walk."

Her gaze followed his to the scattered wrappings she'd discarded along with blood-soaked gauze pads. "Sure. You're right."

"You know how often you say that?" he joked.

She gave him a weak smile before picking up after herself. He didn't offer to help. Bending over wouldn't feel great at the moment.

Five minutes later, she insisted on lifting Garrett's pack so he could shrug into it as easily as possible, then held out his rifle for him to slide his arm inside the strap. She helped position the thing before picking up her own pack. It felt heavier than it had when they started the day.

"The other people who crossed paths with these guys were even luckier than we knew."

"If this Jeff Yonker was more than a rookie, he should have known better than to confront two men carrying the kind of weapons they are."

"From what the friend said, it might have been Evan that worried him," Cadence said.

He grunted, resettled the pack on his back and said, "You ready?"

"Anytime."

As they started out, she wanted to know if he'd seen Evan, and he told her about the flash of red he'd guessed was the boy's sweatshirt. "We already know he's still with them."

"Yes." Cadence sounded subdued. She stayed quiet for quite a while after that, despite earlier seeming to want to talk. In truth, unless they were to talk about themselves, what was there to say?

They did find a sawed-off part of a log that appeared to have been positioned to provide a bench of sorts at the crook of one of the switchbacks. Reluctant to take off his pack, Garrett asked if she had ibuprofen handy and swallowed three tablets when she produced them. He wasn't hungry, but she insisted he eat something, so he downed a couple of handfuls of peanuts.

He was finding the trek down to the narrow valley floor

tougher than the climb to First Divide had been. No surprise there, given to the pain wrapping his torso and the burn and ache in his bicep. If Cadence noticed that he was moving noticeably slower than usual, she didn't comment. These had been a stressful couple of days; she probably wasn't feeling at her peak, either.

Garrett briefly pointed out where he'd encountered the men. She stopped to stare in shock at the raw slices on the trunks of old trees, the chips and broken branches and even a place that a bullet had scraped rock.

After a minute, she wrinkled her nose. "A good ranger would hunt for any cartridges and bullets. Not the kind of thing we want littering this country."

"No, but figuring out where all those bullets went…" He shook his head. "The head ranger can send someone out here later if he feels inclined."

She made a face, but walked on without argument. It had to be five minutes before she said, "I can't imagine how you survived that." So her mind had stayed on the scene behind them. Any chance she'd been scared for him?

"Quick reflexes. I dived for the ground, rolled, got behind some trees."

"And you were wearing a vest."

He glanced at her. "They can be miserable, but when you need it, you need it."

Mostly, they quit talking as they neared the intersection with the Duckabush River. That seemed like a good place for a break…but he stayed uneasily aware of how close he and she followed the men who hadn't hesitated to gun down more people who probably couldn't have done more than annoy them.

As they reached the tumbling river, he speculated on whether *they* stopped here, too. He eyed the ford that consisted of scattered rocks, guessing nobody crossed the river without getting wet to their ankles. The steep flanks of Mount Anderson rose right across the river. Glaciers weren't far above them. A stream that was more a series of waterfalls tumbled down to join the river. It was probably one of countless similar streams created from melting snow that fed these headwaters of the Duckabush River.

Now came time to decide which way to turn, although he knew the decision probably wouldn't be theirs to make. Cadence might be keeping track in her head of where other searchers would be about now, but the picture had grown fuzzy for him. The incident commander—the head ranger, last Garrett knew—would have a map in front of him and might even be moving tacks along the trails for a clear picture. Once they let him know where they were, the call would be his.

If they turned west, they wouldn't have to ford the river. East, they would have to. If anybody asked for preferences, his would be west, on a trail that climbed to O'Neil Pass and led to a series of lakes that were supposed to be beautiful. Ultimately, both choices were part of a kind of loop that encompassed Mount La Crosse and White Mountain.

He had a brief vision of camping tonight at Marmot or Hart Lake, and maybe stripping to immerse himself in cold, astonishingly clear water. The day wasn't hot, but, man, that would feel good.

Yeah, assuming he and Cadence had been here for recreational reasons. Garrett reluctantly banished the fantasy.

"Nobody in their right mind would take the route heading up to La Crosse Pass," Cadence said suddenly. "I mean, we've agreed they're probably not backwoodsmen. A scramble like that… Wearing boots with inadequate tread…"

"Would they know it's a scramble?" Garrett had been thinking about this. "On the topo map, you can see the elevation gain and the little zigzags that make up the trail. I haven't looked at the less detailed one given out to tourists by rangers, but if that's all they have, does it even hint at what they'd be facing?"

"I...don't remember." She promptly dug in her pack, and had to keep digging until she came up with the much skimpier map. "No," she said immediately. "It just looks like a trail. And a short one to cut over to their choice of the Quinault River trail going southwest or the West Fork Dosewallips going northeast. They surely couldn't be imagining they could make it all the way to Hurricane Ridge and become lost in the sea of tourists."

For many visitors to the area, a drive up to Hurricane Ridge and a few minutes appreciating the spectacular view was the closest they'd ever come to the glorious mountains, deep valleys, countless rivers and even a glacier or two that made up the Olympic National Park.

"Hell," Garrett said aloud. "I don't suppose that part of the park has been closed."

"No, doing that would have been premature. Still would be. I mean, Hurricane Ridge is a super long hike away from here."

"True." He let out a breath, grimaced at the sharp pain that lanced his chest. "You ever taken the trail over La Crosse Pass?"

She shook her head. "I hear it's awful from this side. Calling it a 'trail' is kind. Really, it's a climb gaining nearly three thousand feet in elevation, if I remember right. It's so steep, it can't exactly be groomed, and last I heard, there were so many blowdowns, hikers had to duck under downed trees or climb over them, plus it's pretty shrubby. Maybe somebody has gotten out there to saw downed trees to clear the way, but this is only June, so I wouldn't count on it." She paused. "It might look like a good place to get off the radar to those guys, though."

"We've agreed they wouldn't know that unless it turns out one of those stolen packs had a better map in it."

"Which is possible."

He groaned. "I'm going to ford the river and see if there's any indication someone else crossed here not very long ago."

"Oh. That's a good idea." She frowned at him. "Why don't you let me do that?"

He shook his head. "I have longer legs than you. I should be able to make it without getting wet."

Her mouth opened, then closed as she decided not to argue. She found a suitable boulder to sit on and eased her pack from her back, setting her rifle near at hand. "Go for it."

What Garrett feared was that these slugs *would* choose the toughest route, because where better to hole up?

Inevitably, one of the already slick rocks midriver wobbled, his foot slipped, and he found himself ankle-deep in water that felt like it should have a skim of ice on it.

He allowed himself the luxury of some serious swearing since Cadence wouldn't be able to hear him, pulled his foot out and shook it before gingerly setting it down on a broader and, he hoped, more solid rock.

Once he reached the other side, he looked carefully for wet tracks. There were some damp places, but he also saw bear tracks. It went without saying that a black bear wouldn't bother tiptoeing from one rock to another to cross.

He yelled back to Cadence, "Undecided!"

Didn't it make sense for the pair of rangers advancing up

the Duckabush River Trail to get assigned to the La Crosse Pass route? Their hike thus far hadn't been nearly as arduous as his and Cadence's. They hadn't been shot at, or had to load the body of a young man in a helicopter.

Garrett didn't like feeling like a pawn someone else was moving around a board, but he'd knowingly accepted a job where he wouldn't have the same relative autonomy he had as a detective with Seattle PD. Being there for Granddad had an importance that made the tedium of routine patrols and the occasional requirement for him to swallow his pride nothing he couldn't handle.

He *shouldn't* be directing his and Cadence's movement now. He knew that—but he was also the only person who knew about her pregnancy. Hurting more than he wanted her to know, he made the river crossing in reverse, slipping again and, of course, getting his dry foot wet.

At least Cadence appeared sympathetic rather than amused. He carefully sat on the rock beside her and told her his observations. "Bear tracks looked fresh. It could have tromped right on top of any other sign."

"Yes." She bounced the radio in her hand. "My gut says they'd go that way, but I don't really know why."

"Maybe because the part of the loop that includes the lakes is meandering and pointless for someone who just wants to get the hell out of the wilderness?"

"That might be it." Her really dark eyes held his. "What do you think?"

"Whoever is approaching on the Duckabush trail should turn there. That makes more sense than sending us."

"Unless they're still too far away."

He grunted his displeasure.

"Grumpy." The corners of her mouth quivered this time.

"Yeah, yeah."

After scrutinizing Garrett, she announced her intention to get out her stove and cook a real meal—or as real as freeze-dried food got. He must look like hell, he thought ruefully.

"Why don't you check in first?" he suggested. He'd have preferred making the call himself, but she was the law enforcement park ranger, having started out in charge. "I'll fire up the stove."

She agreed, and moments later he heard her giving her call sign and location. Garrett could only hear her side of the conversation, but that was enough for him to know he wouldn't be setting eyes on the idyllic lakes, not this trip.

Chapter Twelve

"What happened to the pair who should be getting close?" he asked, the minute she set down the radio.

"Nothing bad. They should be behind us once we start the ascent. The thing is, the two rangers who were already in Enchanted Valley are taking the loop toward Marmot Lake."

"The helicopter?"

She'd been wondering herself why she hadn't heard it. "Had to fly to the hospital, then refuel. They'll be back soon, which may or may not do any good. I know there are meadows up near the pass, but we'll be closed in by forest for a good part of the ascent."

The lines in Garrett's forehead deepened, but she wasn't sure how much of that had to do with facing what would be a strenuous hike slash climb, and how much because of pain he was keeping quiet about.

"About the time they'd be useful, they'll need to head back to base to beat nightfall."

"Oh, come on! It's only lunchtime." She looked down to see that she'd chosen the menu and put water on to boil. Fine time to realize she wasn't the slightest bit hungry. In fact, her stomach did a roll at the idea of eating the chili she'd picked without thought. Garrett would have been less likely to notice she wasn't eating if they'd grazed on nuts and dried fruit, the way they had other days. On the other hand, he didn't look his sharpest, so maybe he wouldn't pay attention.

Sure.

He seemed to be gazing fixedly at the water, which wasn't in any hurry to boil. *A watched pot*, she thought facetiously.

"You carry a picture of your family?" he asked, out of the blue.

She had no trouble understanding why he was interested, when he'd never been before. Without a word, she took her phone from an outside pocket of her pack and called up photos and then favorites. For a moment, she studied the picture of the four of them that she especially treasured. Her father had his arm around her mother, while each had laid their free hand on one of their children's shoulders. It felt like a circle of love, however sappy that sounded. Simon didn't often like being touched, but he was smiling at her in this photo, looking completely happy.

Along with the squeeze of love, Cadence felt faint apprehension. They'd support her. Of course they would. That didn't mean her plan to raise a baby on her own wouldn't... not disappoint them, just make them feel sad.

A little apprehensive, she handed the phone to Garrett and watched him study it. What he'd see was a plump, blue-eyed, blonde mom; a stocky brown-haired man; Cadence, who didn't look anything like either of them; and her brother, who was mixed race but identified as black. He'd also see that Simon appeared to be in his mid-to-late-twenties.

Garrett blinked a couple of times. "You're adopted."

"Yes. So is Simon, obviously."

"He still lives at home?"

"He's autistic."

His too-perceptive blue eyes now inspected *her*.

"He's on the functional end of the spectrum," she babbled on. "He has an AA degree, a job and friends, but he's happy living at home, and Mom and Dad are happy having one of us still home."

"Huh." Garrett went back to studying the photo as if he could see more than a picture of four smiling people could possibly reveal.

Or maybe it revealed even more than she'd realized.

"You make me see what a coward I've been," he said so quietly she wasn't sure he'd meant for her to hear.

What did he mean? What could she possibly say?

Startled to realize that the water was boiling—of course it was, because both had quit watching it—she held out her hand. Without further comment, he laid the phone in it, the touch of his fingers making her shiver. She closed out photos and dropped the phone in the same pocket before concentrating on pouring the two mixes of freeze-dried chili into the water. She busied herself stirring, then dished it up, hoping he didn't notice what a disproportionate share she served him.

"You made this?" he asked, his pleasant tone reinforcing her impression that, as far as he was concerned, any talk about their childhoods was finished.

"Yes. It's a favorite of mine."

He accepted the pan and a spoon, but hadn't taken a bite when he lifted his head and his gaze speared her.

"Do you know anything about your birth mother?" he asked after a few bites.

She looked away, although not really taking in the view of the river, a deer and a fawn drinking from it and a fish jumping. "My mom left a note when she signed away her parental rights. Said she couldn't take care of me. Whoever was doing intake asked some questions about health concerns that might be passed on, and she claimed there was nothing like that. She wouldn't—or couldn't—answer questions about my father."

"You ever think about looking for her?"

She bent her head over her bowl and swallowed bile. Usually, she loved the spicy aroma, but not now—and especially not when talking about the woman who had given her up with no more than a quick note saying she was sorry. Having a baby couldn't help but open the door to worries about her unknown genetic heritage.

But she said strongly, "No. Why would I? I have the best parents in the world. I didn't miss a thing."

Feeling a sudden misgiving, Cadence sneaked a sidelong glance to see that Garrett was eating with a single-mindedness that suggested he really wasn't thinking about anything else. She didn't believe that for a minute.

"I'm sorry," she said softly. "I imagine you wish your mother *had* surrendered her rights."

He was quiet longer than she liked before saying, "By the time I was old enough to think anything like that, it was too late. Nobody adopts ten-year-olds who are in trouble all the time, or thirteen-year-olds who already top six feet. Once I had to start shaving…" He shrugged. "Not quite what adoptive parents are looking for."

There were people out there who saw deeper than he implied—her parents hadn't hesitated to adopt and love a mixed-race child whose father hadn't been able to deal with a son who recoiled from his touch. Of course, Simon had been only four, but look at Garrett now. Tall, athletic, incredibly handsome, smart, determined…oh, she could go on and on. Surely people should have been able to see behind his youthful, angry facade!

Not that he'd had a chance, when his mother insisted on reappearing in his life just often enough to keep it unsettled.

"It was all a long time ago." Whether he was as indifferent as he sounded, Cadence couldn't tell. He glanced at her untouched bowl and raised his eyebrows.

She almost went with, *I'm not hungry*, but why bother? He already knew about her queasiness. She hadn't admitted that it struck throughout the day when she least expected it, but how could she hide it when they were together 24/7?

"Seconds?" she offered, holding out the bowl.

"You sure?"

"Yes. I'll nibble as we walk. I wasn't thinking when I decided on chili."

He took the bowl, downed her share without commenting on the state of her stomach, thank goodness, and said, "You cooked, I'll clean."

Grateful for the offer, she prepared to get back on the trail. Garrett handed her the stove and dishes to stow in her pack.

"We shouldn't have taken so long," she said.

"I think we both needed a break. Plus, with luck it gives our various backup teams a chance to get in position to do some good."

She smiled at his acid tone. "You know, these guys might be charging on down the Duckabush Trail, and it's Don Phillips and Erik Sorensen who'd come face-to-face with them."

"They know that's a possibility?" He sounded sharp.

Cadence said, "All of us are supposed to be prepared. It just happens you're the one who came the closest."

He made one of his noncommittal noises and swung his

pack onto his back without waiting for help. If it hurt, you'd never know from his expression. She handed over his rifle, slung her own over a shoulder, and they walked the short distance to the ford.

GARRETT WOULD HAVE liked to extend a hand to Cadence so she'd have some support as she made her way gingerly from rock to rock, but was well aware how surprised she'd be. She had considerably more backcountry experience than he did. Without making it obvious, she'd led their previous expeditions into the heart of the park. Unless he'd seen her falling, it wouldn't have occurred to him back then to play the gentleman. Of course, in part this wave of protectiveness came from knowing she was pregnant.

That was *his* baby she carried.

He heard her say, *No, it's* mine, and winced.

Mostly, though, he worried because she wasn't eating enough, because she was too pale, because she wasn't hiding the stress she felt as well as she probably thought she was. Garrett didn't like seeing Cadence as anything but the confident, capable, serene woman he knew her to be. If he could lessen that stress…but he couldn't, and the last thing he wanted to do was undermine her.

She wobbled, held both arms out as she teetered…and found her balance. He wasn't paying enough attention to where he was putting his own foot and slipped.

"Damn," he muttered. This water was *cold*.

Just ahead of him, Cadence played leapfrog and made it to the far bank of the river, boots and feet dry.

He stopped long enough to check to be sure his socks weren't soaked enough to cause discomfort and even blisters, then grinned at her. "You're a ballerina."

She chuckled, her expression easing for a moment. "Your feet are too big."

"That's it. How could I help myself?" Since he wore a size twelve, she had a point.

They moved in concert along the well-groomed trail that followed the Duckabush River. Garrett had guesstimated that it would be three miles, give or take a little, before they reached the La Crosse Pass cutoff. He also knew the La Crosse trail was an additional six and a half miles, a figure that was deceptive, given the extreme elevation gain and loss. Plus… He did a little adding. They'd started with a three–mile round trip from the campsite back to the spur leading to Mount Hopper and then retracing their steps. Two and a half to three miles from First Divide down to the river where they'd just eaten lunch. Never mind the shuddering on the way that included a dead man and bullets flying. The mileage alone added up to… Eight and a half miles, approximately, before they turned off this pleasant, level trail to begin what sounded like a grueling ascent unless the park had gotten some workers out here with chain saws to cut up all the fallen trees and clear the way. Not far for either of them on a usual hike, but…

Given the delays, the sun was still high but noticeably on its way down. Yeah, the day was long, but he'd also noticed some thin clouds he didn't like the looks of. Given the dry winter, rain would be welcome. Not so welcome for a pair of tired hikers trying to catch up with two killers and their hostage.

They were well on their way when he drew Cadence's attention to the clouds. "Those look like rain to you?"

She studied the sky. "Maybe. It's hard to say. If so, it might not come until tomorrow."

"Okay." He waved her ahead, wanting to evaluate her

condition. "Next time you're on the radio, why don't you ask about the weather report?"

"Will do." Her strides were long; he didn't see any sign she was flagging. He also hadn't seen, or heard, any indication she'd had so much as a bite to eat.

He maintained his awareness but felt sure the gunmen weren't hiding along here. The densely forested land to one side climbed at a pitch that made him wonder who had decided a trail heading straight up it was a good idea. The river to their right created a pleasant ripple, and from time to time they saw deer, including a doe with two fawns having a drink. A black bear who stood in the river—fortunately, closest to the other bank—appeared to be fishing, but lifted its massive head to watch them pass. Birds aplenty sang and occasionally spread wings and darted within their sight. Cadence had tried to teach him which birds were which, but he hadn't been an A student. There were so many, and a quick glimpse of outstretched wings didn't tell him if it was a Townsend's warbler versus another kind of warbler, a thrush, a northern flicker or a brown creeper. In another mood, at another time, he'd have asked.

His mood darkened further at the reminder of their purpose and awareness of how soon they'd turn off the trail and begin the scramble that would take them up nearly three thousand feet in elevation in not much over two miles. The abused muscles in his torso spasmed at the mere thought.

When they reached the cutoff, he was encouraged to see that the sign appeared to have been recently replaced. With luck, that meant some real work had been done this spring and early summer on the route.

The initial stretch once he and Cadence turned their backs on the Duckabush River was flat enough, he'd call it a terrace. Old-growth hemlocks towered over them, shutting off sunshine. Now Garrett swept his gaze from side to side, his uneasiness like an itch he couldn't quite reach. As a cop, he knew that feeling too well.

Whether Cadence's unease had increased, Garrett didn't know, only that she wasn't talking. They began the climb, the forest around them changing to a lush mix of silver fir and hemlock, with an understory of ferns, vine maples and devil's club, appropriately named. He'd had an encounter with the spiny leaves one of his first times hiking in the park, and took care now not to brush against one.

Evidence that a chain saw had been used to clear the trail was immediately evident. Large trees had fallen, ripping their roots out of the ground. With the trunks cut to create openings, the scent of evergreen needles and sawdust was sharp in Garrett's nose. Salal had been crushed by the fallen trees. Branches, cut from the trees, had been tossed carelessly into piles. The trail would have been damn near impassible if this much work hadn't been done.

Even Garrett's legs began to burn from the steep climb, but Cadence continued to move with seeming effortlessness. He took a moment to savor her long, slim legs from behind, wishing her bulky pack didn't prevent him from seeing her sleek, dark hair bundled at her nape, as she so often wore it when working. The feel of that hair slipping between his fingers made them tingle now.

She made an exclamation that broke into his thoughts, which she wouldn't have appreciated.

"What…?" He didn't have to complete the question. It appeared the trail work hadn't progressed far at all. A massive tree lay right in front of them, blocking their way. Torn branches might have been planned as an obstacle.

"Damn."

She gave him a sidelong eye roll. "I think we can get under if we take our packs off."

With his larger body, he'd have to squirm like a snake, and he didn't like the possibility of being gashed by the sharp end of one of those broken branches hidden in the dirt. "I think I'd rather go over."

Cadence said, "Hold my pack?"

He took her rifle first, rested it against the trunk, then accepted the weight as she shrugged out of her pack. He couldn't prevent himself saying, "Be careful," as she dropped to her knees.

She was able to mostly crawl beneath the fallen tree, lowering herself at one point to press forward. He saw her butt waggle, then her booted feet, and she was through. Her head just reappeared above the trunk of the tree.

"Ready for your pack?" he asked, and she nodded.

He pushed it, and she pulled. It met resistance, then suddenly popped from his hand. He sent the rifle after it, then eyed the tree. He calculated a route to climb, using stubs where branches had broken off as well as intact ones, and began to climb. He grimaced at the feel of sticky pitch on his hand, but kept going, glad when Cadence came fully into his sight.

He was able to stand upright atop the tree trunk, but any hope of a decent view ahead died a quick death. The zigzagging line on the map perfectly described the route ahead of them. He couldn't see past the next turn.

Normally, he'd have considered jumping, but with his torso already complaining about the scramble, he didn't dare. Just as well—it wouldn't be safe, anyway, given that he could land on a hidden rock or ground soft enough to throw him off-balance. A broken ankle would be a disaster.

He chose to lower his pack and rifle to her, then clamber carefully down. Reclaiming the pack, Garrett knew one thing: he didn't like Cadence in the lead. If there were any surprises facing them, *he* intended to be the one to bear the brunt.

Chapter Thirteen

That first fallen tree was only a foretaste of what was ahead.

A couple of vicious storms had struck the Olympic Peninsula this past winter, near—hurricane force winds sending ocean waves slamming into cliffs along the coast, spray rising frighteningly high. Cadence had stayed in a cabin at Kalaloch once during a storm and enjoyed watching the turbulent ocean throwing new drift logs high up onto the beach. The following morning, she and the other guests at the rustic resort had been able to find all kinds of treasures strewn on the beach, including, in her case, an increasingly rare glass Japanese float that now sat in her closet, for lack of space. That storm, she knew, had been nothing to the later battering that had done this much damage inland. She knew what could happen even in forests that had stood for a thousand years. She just hadn't been able to picture it.

Looking at a couple of trees in front of them that had tumbled one atop the other with so many scattered branches, she thought of the game Pick Up Sticks.

Hands on his hips, Garrett glared at the mess as if it was a personal affront.

"Do you really think they'd keep going once they see what a mess this is?" Cadence asked. He'd know what she meant by "they."

His chest rose and fell with a deep breath. "Yeah, I think it's ideal for their purposes. Nobody can see them from above—"

"Or from twenty feet away," she muttered.

"If they need to stop, they could crawl under a tangle of branches, burrow into the salal and ferns, and who would notice them?"

"Evan—" She bit her lip.

She felt his gaze resting on her face, but didn't let herself look to see what he was thinking.

"A scrawny kid like that, and an athlete, can squirm through a mess like this, no problem. It sucks for us bigger guys who never did gymnastics and don't want to."

She felt a tiny bubble of humor. "Really? I can see you on the rings. You're strong enough for that. Twisting and flipping in the floor exercise, though..."

"It definitely wasn't my sport."

She knew he'd played football both in high school and for the University of Washington, a top program, but hadn't been drafted into the pros. When he'd told her about it, on one of the rare occasions he'd talked about his younger self, he'd said he hadn't been interested, big money or not. He had gone straight to the police academy, as he'd intended since he'd been fifteen or sixteen.

What he hadn't told her was what had happened to him to light the fire of his determination to go into law enforcement. In her case, it had been all but accidental. For him, it was something else altogether, maybe having to do with the time he'd spent with his mother, maybe even living on the street.

She shook off her curiosity. He hadn't talked about it to her because he didn't want her to get to know him well, any more than he'd wanted to plumb her depths. Except...

she had a feeling that now, if she asked him, he'd answer. He seemed determined to lower barricades, even if they creaked as if rusty. She wanted to feel hope.

Now was not the time. What she needed to do was focus on how to make her way under, over and between the current obstacles.

As before, she mostly squirmed through gaps, while Garrett climbed over the top. Of course that made sense, given the breadth of his shoulders and his height, but she also wondered how much his decisions were made by his pain level—the one he implied was next to nonexistent.

Typical man.

She wrinkled her nose. Not like she appreciated whiners.

Impeding both of them were the Kevlar vests that added bulk to their torsos. Evan wouldn't have that handicap, either.

They toiled through several more obstacles before taking a short break. Garrett dug out some snack foods from his pack and handed them to her with an expression that said she'd better eat or else. He got on the radio, only to have to wait in increasing frustration as other talk dominated. Apparently a nasty domestic dispute had erupted at the Elwha RV campground, which was momentarily at the forefront of the dispatcher's attention. Another ranger was behind a speeder on Highway 101 along the coast and wanting more information on a license plate number.

Cadence nibbled while Garrett swigged water and listened until he heard at least some of what he wanted to know, it seemed.

"Did you get that?" he said finally. "Phillips and Sorensen—I assume you know them?—aren't far from us, and the rangers that were in the Enchanted Valley are approaching the other end of the trail.

"Oh. That's Nathan Ryback and Davis Bourke. They're good."

"Maybe we should wait."

"No!" she cried. "We're quieter on our own."

His mouth tightened, but he nodded.

"All right. I'll concede as much. We'd better silence our radios from here on out and keep conversation to a minimum."

"They've got to be quite a way ahead of us."

"Do they? They're not woodsmen, remember? And who knows what they're thinking at this point?"

He was right, of course. Would Evan seize an opportunity and try to escape? She didn't know if she hoped he did or not. What she felt certain of was that those men wouldn't shrug and let him go. They'd shoot him. They sure hadn't hesitated when the two climbers dared question them, or when they realized Garrett was pursuing them. Evan's youth wouldn't deter them, she felt sure.

Cadence wanted this all to be over with. To restore Evan to his family, watch the two men get hauled off in handcuffs and wave goodbye to Garrett in the Staircase parking lot.

Well, maybe not the goodbye part even if it would surely be the reality, despite the effort he was making.

Anyway, she thought ruefully, they wouldn't be able to hike out today. Whether they accomplished an arrest or not, there would be another night together. A chance for a chivalrous Garrett to press her to do what she longed for, deep inside: to marry him, to lull herself into believing he was capable of loving her and their child, of never regretting a commitment.

Accepting less than she needed and deserved would surely be a terrible mistake.

She wrapped the dried banana chips she hadn't finished

and dropped the packet into a pocket. "We'd better get going."

"Yeah." He inspected her with those unnervingly sharp eyes. "You've acquired some scratches."

"I'm aware. They do sting. You have some, too."

He lifted a finger to a scrape on his forehead that was beaded with droplets of blood, touched it and came away with a bloody fingertip. "Not worth cleaning up until we get past this section. I may have words with your boss when we get back."

She shook her head. "You know how underfunded all the parks are, right? It's getting worse all the time."

He let out a long breath. "I do know that. Under normal circumstances, we could call this an adventure. But today…"

She didn't say anything. He groaned, leaned back to shrug on his pack and waited to pick up his rifle until she was ready to go. Then he set out, leaving her to follow.

IT WAS ALL very well to start in the lead, but several times Cadence slipped through the downed hemlocks or firs ahead of him and emerged on her own. Garrett hated every minute he lost sight of her.

As tedious as all this was, he found his mind occasionally wandering. If he'd brought a handsaw, he could have at least lopped off some of the limbs to make it easier for the next hiker without slowing himself down much.

He couldn't believe she had flat out refused to marry him, now that she was pregnant. Just because he hadn't been able to say the words, *I love you*, did she believe he'd walk out on her? Or cheat on her? Didn't she know what the changes he'd made in his life to support the grandfather he hadn't known all that well meant about who he was? And hadn't she noticed how cheap the easily spoken words, *I love you*, too often were? She'd said herself, the two of them were solid together. If he was able to love a woman, Cadence would have been the one. He'd already acknowledged that much to himself. He'd hated losing her. Even before he knew she was pregnant, the idea of never seeing her again had shaken him. He tried to be honest with himself, but it had taken days before he admitted as much.

Once this operation was over, he'd press her on the subject. He could be stubborn. She'd see that marrying made sense. No way was he willing to be an occasional father!

The sound of a branch snapping ahead sharpened his focus. Cadence was already in the act of wedging herself under the latest blowdown, but had miscalculated. It hadn't been a real big branch, though, he saw; nothing that would have injured her.

"Hold up," he said, suddenly in the moment. "Don't get ahead of me."

Her response was a breathless, "There isn't room for both of us."

"Then let me go ahead."

"Don't be silly. I'm almost through. You should be able to make it under this time, too."

He thought so, too. Laid his rifle on the forest floor and pushed it through behind her, then lowered himself to his hands and knees. When he started, he could see her legs from this perspective, but she took a few steps and he lost sight of her.

With sudden urgency, he called, "Cadence!"

A cry came from her.

The alarm made him careless. His pack snagged on a sharp stub of a snapped-off branch.

The next muffled cry from her sounded like she was trying to say his name—or to warn him.

That rumble had to be a man's voice. Feeling as if he was moving in slow motion, Garrett tore himself from his pack and grabbed at the rifle even as he threw himself forward. What he saw was his worst fear.

A brawny man was wrenching Cadence up a gritty slab of rock to the side of the trail. She fought him, literally tooth and nail. The boy was struggling against a second man waiting higher up.

Garrett yanked hard at the rifle, but resistance meant that strap was snagged, too.

After her teeth sank into the creep's bicep, he slugged her. Her head snapped to one side. Somehow, she still reached high and took hold of the young boy's arm, tearing him free from his captor at the top of the slab. Face contorted with fear, the boy slid uncontrollably on his butt. Cadence got out a "*Run*, Evan!" before a meaty hand covered her mouth and wrenched her head back.

Sweating, filled with rage, Garrett gave up on the rifle, unsnapped the holster and pulled his Glock. Still on his stomach, he reached out to brace his grip with both hands.

The delay was enough to let the vicious guy all but throw her up into the arms of the second man crouched at the top of the slab. Then he got a hand on Evan as he slid past, pulling him up as a shield. Garrett's shot was riskier than he liked, but…

Free the boy. That's what Cadence would want, what she'd fought for rather than trying to get away herself.

Flung into the cold space that was his norm when he had to make quick decisions and fire his weapon, Garrett's hands stayed steady as he aimed for the shoulder that was too broad to hide behind the lanky kid. He pulled the trigger once. Blood blossoming on his upper arm, the man re-coiled. Garrett pulled the trigger again.

Evan fell free and rolled down almost to Garrett's feet. The son of a bitch above barely hesitated before lunging over the lip and disappearing. Garrett's last sight of him he'd clapped a hand to his gory arm. His shooting arm, Garrett sincerely hoped.

They had Cadence. He couldn't let himself think of everything they might do to her.

"Let's get out of sight." He pushed the kid ahead to squeeze past his pack and get behind the one fallen tree. Unsnagging rifle and pack on the way, he followed, standing on the other side. His voice was harsh. "Are you hurt, Evan?"

"I...don't know." Confusion and fear showed in hazel eyes. "Who was she?"

Was. Past tense. Garrett shut down the snarl that wanted to form.

"Cadence Jones. Park ranger and—" *My partner. My lover. The mother of my baby.* He couldn't say any of that. "We've been following you since they kidnapped you at the Staircase campground. I'm Jefferson County Deputy Garrett Wycoff. Sit down here and let me take a look at you."

His skin felt too tight as his instincts screamed for him to go after her. Now. He felt a pull that was hard to resist. The kid would be all right waiting for the others, he tried to convince himself.

No, he had to make sure.

The boy's teeth chattered. "Who *are* they?"

Garrett summarized everything that had occurred since the gun shop robbery. "They knew a hostage might be all that would save them."

Eyes watery, Evan whispered, "But...now they have *her.*"

"Yeah."

He put the boy through a basic set of motions, and determined his skinned back from the uncontrolled slide down the rough rock slab was his worst injury. Garrett eased that red sweatshirt over Evan's head, sprayed his back with some painkiller, gently laid on salve and covered it all with a clean T-shirt he dug out of the bottom of his pack. Best he could do. Cadence would have had better supplies, but at his last sight she still had her pack with her. Then, seeing the boy shaking, he added one of his flannel shirts, rolling the sleeves until the kid's hands actually poked out.

"They been feeding you?" he asked.

"Um…sort of."

Garrett handed over water first, then snack foods and watched the kid eat like there was no tomorrow. He remembered too well those years when he was growing like Jack's beanstalk and was starved all the time.

Then, reluctant, he took out the radio. He hoped like hell the pair hadn't yet investigated Cadence's pack and discovered *her* radio. But he couldn't send an eleven-year-old boy down the trail or leave him sitting here alone, without rangers Phillips and Sorensen knowing they'd be coming upon him. Garrett couldn't take a chance that one of them would get trigger-happy when they saw movement. Also, he couldn't justify leaving Evan's grandparents and other family in agonizing suspense.

But he had no intention of hanging around for long, not when it meant letting those bastards get more lead than they already had.

CADENCE TASTED BLOOD in her mouth and gritted her teeth against the pain as one of her kidnappers threw her forward on rocky ground. She made the mistake of trying to control the fall. She knew better; she should have twisted instead of catching her weight on the heels of her hands. Her wrists felt as if she'd broken them, and a shock wave rolled up her arms to her shoulders. Her palms stung.

The man who was bleeding lifted her handgun from her holster, glanced at it and dropped it into one of their packs. Standing above her, his expression ugly, he snapped, "Don't think you can slow us down, bitch!"

The buddy grabbed her arm and yanked her to her feet, hard enough that she couldn't prevent a pained sound from escaping. On top of everything else, she felt as if he might have dislocated her shoulder.

They were big guys, somewhere around Garrett's height of six foot three. Over her head, they had an angry, obscenity-laden exchange. From it she determined that their names were Cole and Mason. Teeth showing in a snarl, Cole clutched the bloody wound at the top of his arm. Along with being mad at the world, they were furious with each other. Both seemed to feel the need to blame the other for their predicament, and why not? It took some maturity to say, *Yeah, we screwed up.* And even more to say, I *made a bad decision. It was* my *fault we took that last disastrous turn.*

If the packs they'd stolen had contained any toiletries like razors or soap and water, there was no sign they'd used them. Those had to be the clothes they'd started in days ago. Both had stubble turning to ragged beards, sweat stains under their arms and filthy cargo pants. Boots…she'd call them work boots, probably with a decent sole but not the kind needed for hiking tough terrain. A picture flashed through her head of the two men whose backpacks these were. They'd been lean and athletic, but not big. No, their clothing wouldn't fit either of these two.

Both these men looked like dedicated weight lifters.

Mason, the larger of the two, had hair that might be blond if he ever washed it again. He aggressively demanded to know how his partner could have lost that scrawny kid.

Cole, the one who'd chosen to hold on to her instead of Evan, gave a one-shoulder shrug. "She's better than the boy." Teeth bared, he looked her over in a way that made her skin crawl. "Nice piece of ass."

The buddy shrugged. "Kinda skinny."

"All the more for me."

Oh, God. Please, please, Cole was trying to scare her, versus being serious. Surely he wouldn't take time to— She didn't get past the image of his thick fingers ripping her shirt off.

She didn't kid herself. He was already wanted for at least two murders. Whatever brakes he'd once had on his behavior would be nonexistent now. *Pedal to the metal.* Her father had used that term.

She could only try to hold out. Hold on to her memory of the way Garrett had called her name, the agony in his eyes before they turned ice-cold when he fired his gun. He might not know how to love, but she believed he would do anything, die in her place if that was the only choice, to save her. This certainty, her trust in him, felt bone-deep, and she had the fleeting thought that maybe she'd misjudged him. Maybe his commitment *would* be powerful enough to make up for the lack of romance.

The thought came and went, lost in the fear as Cole demanded she put on *his* pack while he took hers, and shoved her ahead on the poor excuse for a trail.

Of course, they almost immediately came to the largest fallen tree yet, an ancient giant she'd have mourned under other circumstances. Mason kicked it and berated her. She was a park ranger, and her *job* was to clear the goddamn trails. What did she do instead, wander around at camp-grounds and tell stories to the kiddies by firelight?

Not a good idea to inform them that, actually, her role in the park was law enforcement. Or that, as the courts would see it, they had kidnapped a federal agent. FBI, DEA, National Park Service, it didn't matter.

She tried very hard to hide the shudder that wracked her. No, as she'd already reminded herself, it *wouldn't* matter to these men who she was. What was one more crime? Nonetheless, she for damn sure wasn't going to mention that the latest kidnappings would mean two trials: one in a federal courtroom, one in a Washington state court.

Mason swung himself over the massive trunk, picking his way and pushing between the unbroken limbs, and disappeared to the other side. Cole shoved her beneath the trunk and waited until his buddy called, "I've got her," before also climbing over. His right hand left bloody smears behind. Holding his injured arm against himself, he mumbled to himself the entire time. He had the foulest mouth she'd ever heard, and that was saying something.

The broken branches as well as the ones still attached were as difficult as the downed trees themselves. They trampled through, whips of fir and cedar branches wrapping around their ankles as if they'd been set as snares. A hard shove from behind sent her crashing down onto something sharp. She didn't see what ripped through her shirt and into her flesh until she whimpered and pushed herself to her hands and knees. The end of a shattered piece of branch, half-driven into the soil, was as sharp as if it had been meant to be a spear.

"Up, up! We don't have time to lie around!" Cole snarled. For all the rage and fear on his broad face, the fact that he still had the control to keep his voice low scared her as much as anything.

As she climbed shakily to her feet, she bent her head to see a long rent in her shirt, blood soaking it and the bra visible through the tear.

Cole pushed her again, and she wheeled to snap, "Stop that unless you want me to keep falling down!"

He leaned in until his face was inches from hers, and then grabbed her left breast. "If you get too mouthy, we won't bother hauling you along. Get that? *This*—" he squeezed her breast painfully hard "—is the only reason I'm being so *patient*."

It was all she could do to hold his stare without cowering. A flash of emotion in his eyes told her he didn't like her lack of reaction.

And wasn't that too bad.

She looked him up and down. "You know, I'm an EMT. I can probably patch you up, if I'm not injured too bad to help anyone else." Without another word, she turned and struggled on behind Mason, who had paused a distance ahead to watch them.

She had no clue which of these men had actually shot the Clallam County deputy or the climbers. Right this second, Mason scared her a little less than the buddy who followed her so closely, his horrible breath all but tickling her neck.

Her stomach turned.

How far behind was Garrett? Or was he still taking care of Evan? *Please hurry*, she begged silently. *Please*.

Because she had to wonder what these two had in mind, given that they had to know a noose was closing around them.

If she saw even the smallest chance to run, she'd have to take her chance.

Chapter Fourteen

Head hanging, Evan mumbled, "It would have been better if they'd kept me."

"What?" Garrett turned his head. "Why would you say that?"

"'Cause they didn't really hurt me." Exhaling, he looked up. "But she's a girl. A woman," he corrected himself. "She'll be easier to hurt."

This was the last conversation in the world that Garrett wanted to be having. But he couldn't let this poor kid get stuck with a major guilt complex because Cadence had essentially traded herself for him. And if the boy hadn't considered the possibility of rape, Garrett wasn't going to raise it.

"No," he said. "They don't know it, but she's a trained law enforcement officer, not just the kind of ranger who gives nature talks. She arrests people regularly. A couple of weeks ago, she brought down a really bad guy who had kidnapped a little girl. I know she looks…" *Delicate*, was how he always thought of her, but said, "Slender. It's deceptive. I've mountain climbed with her. She's strong. Plus, if she can get her hands on a gun, I'm betting she's a better shot than either of those two." He tried for a grin that had to be crooked. "They look like they're better at lifting weights than they are at using their heads."

"Yeah! I mean, how do they think they're going to get away from *here*?"

"I suspect they keep thinking a hostage is all they need, but they're wrong," Garrett said grimly.

Evan's eyes widened. "You mean, like, if they threaten to kill her, the cops would say, do it? We're still not letting you go?"

Nobody had better say anything resembling that in Garrett's hearing range. He breathed deeply. "If we say it, we won't mean it. Really, what will probably happen is that we'll make promises to those men that we won't keep. We'll convince them to believe they can still pull this off, when really they don't have a chance. And I suspect we won't even have to do that. I'm betting Ranger Jones either escapes, or brings them down on her own."

The hope on the boy's face hurt to see. Garrett wished he believed his own words.

"Wow! She must be really something."

"Yeah." He cleared his throat. "She is."

"Deputy? That you?" a man called from a short distance down the trail.

Garrett stood. "It is. You Phillips or Sorensen?"

"We're both here."

Within moments the men came into sight, their appearances more reassuring than Garrett had anticipated. Both were, like Cadence, law enforcement rangers. Neither seemed as if the maddening obstacles on the trail had hampered them in any meaningful way. Garrett felt sure he was a lot scruffier at this point. One of the two had significant gray in his hair, but looked strong despite carrying a hefty pack and a rifle. The other guy was younger but had the same air of confidence.

Of course, it was easy to be confident when the woman in such peril wasn't everything to *them*.

Garrett felt the ground beneath his feet shift, but he couldn't acknowledge it. Not here and now.

He held out his hand. "Garrett Wycoff."

They shook hands all around, Evan watching warily.

Garrett told them what had happened in more detail than he'd shared over the radio, then said bluntly, "I'd like one of you to take Evan back down. I know it's late in the afternoon, but once you're on an open trail, you might want to call in and see if a helicopter can pick him up." He squeezed the boy's shoulder. "I suspect his family would like to have him back as soon as possible."

Don Phillips smiled at the boy. "I hear your mom and dad drove over and are waiting at the campground with your grandparents. There might have been something about two sisters, too."

Evan scrunched up his nose, but said, "A helicopter? Really? That might be cool."

Phillips raised his eyebrows at Garrett. "You've been on this a lot longer than we have. I gather you were shot."

"Nothing significant." It was obvious where the guy was going with this, and it wasn't happening.

"Maybe you should take Evan and let us step up now."

"No. Cadence is my partner. We were—" he hesitated and settled for "—friends. We've done some climbing together. I can't walk away."

The younger ranger spoke up. "We're both pretty well acquainted with her, too."

"She has her radio with her. I'm assuming they'll use it to get in touch. I'm former Seattle PD. I've had training as a negotiator. Along with that, I also know Cadence well enough to read between the lines if she's able to tell us what she thinks we need to know."

The two men glanced at each other, Phillips finally nodding. "I've attended workshops on negotiating, but I can't call that real training. I gather that some rangers have started up this trail from the West Fork Dosewallips River end already. Unless the men we're pursuing pull a rabbit out of a hat, we have to be heading toward a standoff. They've got to be tired. If you can drag things out while keeping Ranger Jones as safe as possible, she might have a chance to make a move—or we can when one of them is asleep."

Garrett nodded. "That's what I'm thinking."

He didn't like envisioning the situation she was in, but it was unavoidable. He had to get into the heads of those two pieces of scum…and read Cadence's mind, too. Until this week, he'd have said avoidance wasn't one of his weaknesses, but he was learning better. What else could he call his refusal to acknowledge what he felt for her?

The two rangers consulted briefly. Without paying a lot of attention, Garrett had the impression that they made the decision to leave Eric Sorensen to partner with him because he was the better shot. *Army trained as a sniper*, he told Garrett. If he was good enough to pick one or both of these scumbags off, Garrett was fine with that. He'd arrested plenty of men or women who he could acknowledge had a core of decency, had had some hard knocks that led to bad decisions, or who deserved sympathy or at least pity from him. The decisions these two had made told him they were bad, plain and simple. Their readiness to shoot and kill anyone at all so they could get out of trouble said enough, but adding on their decision to grab a kid as hostage…?

His molars ground together. And now Cadence. What she might be enduring...

He *couldn't* let himself imagine too much, or he'd lose it. He had to stay clearheaded for her sake. And right this minute, not much else mattered but Cadence.

After hearing Garrett had fired his handgun, Phillips gave him a spare magazine.

"I'll rejoin you two if I can get a pickup for Evan." He smiled at the boy. "I hope I can, instead of making you walk all the way out. *And* spending another night on the way."

Evan looked close to tears that he didn't want to embarrass himself by sharing. Garrett cuffed him lightly on the back.

"Remember, Ranger Jones made her choice. You were her biggest worry. Knowing you're safe and on your way back to your family will be a weight off her mind. I promise."

The boy's Adam's apple bobbed. "You'll let me know? I mean, what happens?"

"Yeah. Here." He took out his mostly useless phone, relieved it had enough juice left to allow him to pull up contacts. "Give me your number, and I'll call you myself when I can."

He entered the number and saved it, then turned off the phone and pocketed it again. "You're a gutsy kid," he said with a nod.

Evan astonished him by giving him a hard hug before sniffing, wiping his nose on the hem of his shirt and starting down the trail. Phillips lifted a hand and followed.

"That's nice, what you said," Sorensen commented after a minute.

Garrett grimaced and told him about Evan's guilt that his safety had come at the expense of Cadence's.

"You're right," the ranger said. "Good heart, too."

Garrett cleared his throat. "Yeah." He felt a hard tug on the line that pulled him toward Cadence. "You ready?"

"When you are."

He'd been ready since that last desperate look he'd shared with Cadence. Without another word, he heaved his pack onto his back, then slung both Cadence's rifle and his own over his shoulder.

CADENCE PRESSED A hand to her torso just beneath her right breast. She hadn't bled copiously enough to worry her, but she had at the least bruised her torso severely, and conceivably cracked or broken a rib.

Garrett and she made a fine pair.

She'd asked to take a minute to clean and bandage the wound, but Cole had, predictably, sneered. *He* was tough enough to handle a bullet wound and didn't give a damn what her problem was.

"Don't think we'll let you drag your feet."

That hadn't been her intent then, but she set out after that to slow them down. Once, she snagged her pack as she scooted under a fallen cedar and required Cole's irritated assistance to free her; the other time, she tripped and went down, groaning and pretending greater difficulty than she felt as she pushed herself back to her feet.

The trail was as steep as guide books warned. Bringing up the rear, Cole breathed like a winded horse. His face was beet red, partly from sunburn, if she had to guess, but otherwise from exertion. The color did not look healthy. If only he'd drop dead from a heart attack, she thought vengefully. Unfortunately, although he'd bled plenty, he wasn't gushing.

Despite *not* being injured, Mason wasn't doing much

better, although he had the sense to save his breath for hiking instead of complaining and swearing constantly. Garrett had been right, Cadence decided; they'd gained those impressive muscles in a gym, not doing an aerobic activity that might have helped them now. Still, they were scared enough to keep moving. If it hadn't already occurred to them, she wasn't going to mention that sometime in the next hour or two, they'd come face-to-face with yet more armed pursuers.

And Garrett... Garrett would be right behind, moving a lot faster than these two did.

The landscape around them changed subtly as they gained elevation. Undergrowth diminished because the trees were closer together. A denser stand meant fewer of them had fallen in the storms, leaving the trail clear for longer stretches. That would have allowed them to move faster, except that the steep climb slowed the pace instead. She was practically walking on Mason's heels, although some of that had to do with the creepy-crawly feelings she had, knowing how close Cole was behind her. Wondering if he was assessing her, imagining what he could do to a helpless woman. She hated knowing that, sooner or later, she'd have to clean up his shoulder and bandage it.

In scattered places that were open enough for the sun to reach the forest floor, she spotted huckleberries...and bears. Cadence kept her mouth shut, wondering if either man had noticed. Apparently not, because it took a roaring, grumbling sound before Mason jerked as if he'd gotten an electrical shock.

"What the...?"

Guarding two cubs, Mama bear was still far enough away, Cadence suspected she was only posturing. Swearing, Mason grabbed his rifle and started to lift it.

"Don't!" Cadence leaped forward and gripped his arm. "If you kill her, the cubs will starve to death."

"Looks like she wants to eat us," he growled.

"No, she's just putting on a show to keep us from approaching. Besides...she's big enough, she'd be hard to bring down. A few bullets would just make her mad."

"Then what does Miss-Know-It-All suggest?" Cole asked, his sarcasm not hiding his fear.

She stepped forward, waved her arms and yelled, "Shoo!"

Mama shuffled back a few feet.

Cadence lowered her voice. "Just keep moving."

They did, the men watching the bear as closely as she watched them. Cadence took satisfaction in seeing the whites of their eyes. She was surprised that they hadn't had previous standoffs with bears. Unless they'd been way farther ahead of her and Garrett than she thought they'd been, she'd have heard the gunfire if they strafed some poor black bear with automatic weapon fire out of ignorance as much as malice.

"Don't want to make the noise anyway," Cole snapped, earning a glare from his friend, who then turned and marched on.

The pause had regulated Cole's breathing, but that didn't last long. As the trail took another switchback, he began puffing again. Likely neither of them appreciated the sight of wild rhododendrons in full bloom, the pink flowers a beautiful contrast to the dark green backdrop.

"Isn't there a pass up here, somewhere?" Mason grumbled.

"You don't know where you're going?" She knew she sounded incredulous.

He clearly didn't like it, wheeling around, his expression dark. "Watch it."

She resisted the desire to shrink back. "Um, La Crosse Pass. It's known for spectacular views."

"Views?" Now he scowled. "Like, we'll be in the open?"

"It's almost high enough to be a mountain summit. I think Mount La Crosse isn't that much higher."

He looked past her. "We've got to find a place to get off the trail and stop. We ought to be able to hide in the trees."

"I wouldn't mind shooting down a helicopter." Despite the heavy breathing, Cole sounded like he meant it.

Could they shoot one down? Even though she'd vaguely thought it would take a rocket grenade or something like that, Cadence had a bad feeling. If fully automatic rifles...

Pretend you're a tour guide, she told herself. *Calm, sharing interesting information.*

"If you did that, you could set off a forest fire. This is... early in the year, but the winter was dry." A serious fire was still unlikely in June, but she wouldn't tell *them* that. "You're not feeling much wind, but if you look up, you'll see the tops of the trees bending."

Both of them tipped their heads back.

"A forest fire leaps from treetop to treetop. It's terrifying. We couldn't outrun it."

"Light's going," Mason observed. "We can hole up for the night."

Wonderful. Why had she opened her big mouth about the glorious view from the highest point this trail reached?

Mason was right, though; in her brief glimpses of the sky, it was shading to violet that would deepen to purple before nightfall. The sun would make an early descent behind the dozen peaks to the west, from Mount Christie to the much nearer White Mountain and Mount La Crosse. If she and Garrett had been hiking for pleasure—her heart compressed at her choice of word—she'd have suggested the same. The hard part would be scrambling across the steep, heavily wooded slope and finding a large enough spot that was flat.

"Left or right?" Cole snapped.

"You're asking me?"

"Who else?"

"I…really don't know. My topographic map shows it equally steep either way. I mean, until you get closer to the top."

"To the pass."

"We'd be almost there once the trail levels out."

"Hell with it." He nodded to the daunting forest to their left, where trees grew at a sharp angle from the ridge.

This might be her chance. A few steps, and she could put some trees between them. She could also break an ankle with the slightest misstep, she thought ruefully.

The two men looked over her head again and came to an apparent, wordless agreement. Looking sullen, Mason started picking his way into the trees, feet skidding. He had to grab for feathery evergreen limbs or rocky outcrops, even wrap his arms around the trunks of smaller trees. Within a few steps, his feet went out from under him and he came down on his knees, swearing viciously.

Hey, they might comprehend the benefit of switchback trails carved laboriously out of the side of a ridge this steep.

Trying to appear casual, Cadence crossed her arms and watched. In reality, she groped with the hand Cole couldn't see to find something, a scrap left from a food packet, an empty evidence bag, *anything*, to drop as a signal to Garrett.

My ring. The thin ring banded from two colors of gold she'd worn on her right hand since her mother gave it to her on her sixteenth birthday. Garrett would recognize it. As long as he spotted it…

Cole shoved her. "Go."

She'd almost worked the ring off her finger. *Drop it in front of herself where he wouldn't see.* What if he did?

She had to take a chance.

Cadence lowered her hand and let the ring fall. It was too obvious there on the trail. Cole would see it. He'd—

She made a production of starting after Mason, tension running up her neck. Was Cole right behind her, or still standing on the trail?

Given experience approaching mountains where no trail had ever been even unofficially established, she moved with more ease at first than the big guy in front of her did. Her better traction helped, as did her much smaller feet. Still, it was really hard going.

A grunt from behind let her know Cole wasn't letting her get far ahead of him. He'd have said something if he'd seen the ring, wouldn't he?

Eventually, she got careless because too much of her brain had turned to plotting. If this happened, what would she do? If that happened instead, how could she take advantage?

What if Mason really fell? If she whirled and rammed Cole, could she knock him down, too? If only she still had her handgun. Waiting until they stopped might give her the chance to get her hands on one of their rifles...

The left toe of her boot hooked on a rock or exposed tree root, and she plunged down, hard. Before she could stop herself, she'd rolled over a six- or eight-foot drop-off and slammed to a stop against a really sizable tree trunk. Her ribs screamed, and she started retching even as she drew her knees up under her.

Idiot! she castigated herself, clutching at her belly and torso, dry heaving.

"What the—?" Venting his usual obscenities, Cole the creep used those overblown muscles to lower himself to her. "You're not that good an actor!"

"I'm not..." she got out between heaves of her stomach.

"You're like a deer," he said in obvious disgust. "If you break a leg and slow us down too much, we'll put you out of your misery."

Gritting her teeth against the agony and the bile that soured her mouth, Cadence felt sure he meant what he was saying. He'd have no compunction about putting his barrel to her head and pulling the trigger. She *had* to get up, keep moving. Garrett couldn't save her, if she didn't save herself first.

Anyway...it wasn't just her anymore. *Baby, I'm sorry*, she thought. *I'll get us out of this. I will*.

Aside from everything else, even if Garrett didn't, couldn't, love her, she knew what finding her dead body and all possibility of their child having a life would do to him.

Groaning, she pushed herself to her hands and knees. "I hit that tree hard. I think my rib might be broken." If it hadn't already been. "But don't worry, I can keep going."

"You'd better." He nudged her with a booted foot, almost knocking her over again. "You're my ace in the hole, so don't do anything stupid."

She bobbed her head. "I won't."

"Then get your butt moving."

Pain increasing tenfold, her stomach somewhere between queasy and outright rebellion, she did what he asked. At least he wouldn't question further nausea when it hit her for a completely different reason.

Chapter Fifteen

Garrett and Eric, now on first name terms, moved more slowly than Garrett would have liked, but he didn't want to miss anything. With daylight beginning to wane, he had trouble believing the pair would march on to the pass. They wouldn't risk being caught out in the open. On the other hand, this steep sidehill didn't suggest a comfy campsite might lie just out of sight.

If they had a topographical map, they'd be able to tell when the elevation gain began to ease and maybe start looking then for a place to stop. If they didn't...

Damn, he hated having to second-guess these bastards at a time when every decision meant so much. What if he and Eric hiked right past the threesome, huddled a mere twenty feet away?

If they did part ways from the trail, would Cadence be able to post a sign for him? Might be easier said than done. She couldn't be obvious, and that was assuming she had anything at all small enough for her to get away with dropping it.

"I think that's the helicopter," Eric said.

Garrett paused and heard the muffled roar. "About damn time."

"Won't be able to see them anyway. Or us, for that matter."

All true, but the presence of the helicopter, which began

making regular passes overhead, put pressure on the two men who didn't dare be glimpsed. How they'd use Cadence in that situation, he didn't like to think, but didn't let himself off the hook.

Don Phillips would be here in his place if anyone running this operation had a clue that Garrett and Cadence had been lovers. If one of his fellow deputies involved had a suspicion, he or she must have kept their mouths shut. Cadence's roommates must have known she was seeing someone, gone overnight or even for two nights a few times, and why wouldn't Cadence have identified him? Yeah, but both were seasonal employees, and from what she'd said, liked to party and had a different social circle than Cadence did. He was lucky, because he couldn't have handled being banned from this hunt.

God, if anyone knew that she carried his baby? He wouldn't so much as be allowed an opinion, much less essentially being in charge of on-scene operations now that Cadence had been snatched.

He had to be more careful what he said.

The light was failing. It was growing harder to pick out details. He'd been determined to pinpoint the exact location where Cadence was being held before stopping for the night. If they were far off the trail, it wouldn't be easy to bring in reinforcements to surround them, though. This was the worst possible terrain for an ambush.

"Damn it," he muttered, just as the younger ranger behind him said, "We'd better start thinking—"

He opened his mouth to agree, but saw a glint on the trail ahead. He lifted his hand in a "wait" gesture and continued, not taking his eyes off whatever he was seeing for an instant. He stopped to crouch, desperately hoping Cadence had left a message and this wasn't nothing but a shred of trash a hiker had dropped without noticing.

The moment he reached his finger out, he knew. It was gold, a ring, and an unusual one at that. He'd never seen anything else like it. Rose gold interrupted the more common gold. Cadence said it had belonged to a great-grandmother. An adoptive great-grandmother, but Cadence had the security of owning her family, of knowing she was *theirs*. That still bemused him.

"What is it?" Eric asked softly, crouching to join him.

"A ring." He picked it up, holding it in his palm. "It's Cadence's. I noticed it and asked about it earlier." Months ago, but he left the implication it had been in the past day or two. "She had to have dropped it here on purpose."

Eric lifted his head and frowned as he looked around. "Which way?"

"It's at the very edge of the trail. I'm going to say that's part of the message."

"Makes sense. So now what do *we* do?"

"They can't have gone far."

Eric didn't say anything.

"Stop right here." And, damn, were those words hard to say.

Hand closing on the ring, he imagined it still held some warmth from her hand. He surveyed the trail. Not anyplace meant for two men to stretch out in comfort, but he suspected no such thing existed until closer to the pass. The sense of an unseen strand connecting him to Cadence seemed to quiver, giving a tug. *This way*, it whispered. No, he didn't intend to lengthen the distance between them by even a few strides if he could help it.

"This is as good as it's going to get." She'd been relieved to see a place where several trees appeared to have sprouted from a nurse log, their trunks now all but grazing each other to form a near wall. The result was soil dammed up above them. "Do either of you have an ice axe?" she asked.

"A *what*?"

She lowered the pack she carried and leaned it against a tree, immediately seeing what she sought. "This," she said. An ice axe was strapped to Cole's pack, the one he'd lifted from the climber. She'd avoided looking at him as much as possible. She was surprised he hadn't discarded the axe, but maybe he'd envisioned it's possibilities as a weapon. It would have made a good walking stick, besides, but the head had a sharp point designed for stabbing into a crack in the rocks or ice to arrest a fall, while the other side widened into a blunt tool for scraping.

After leaning her pack against a tree, Cadence demonstrated how this ground could be leveled, then continued since neither man volunteered to take over the task. *She* couldn't help envisioning what she could do with that sharp steel point. She imagined herself turning fast, already swinging. That steel point would easily crack open a head. She made herself picture the moment of impact, the sound of a skull splitting, and her queasiness increased. She'd never actually killed anyone before, and had hoped never to have to do so. Especially in such a gruesome way. But if that was the only way she could save herself and her unborn child, she couldn't let herself be squeamish.

Her muscles tightened.

How fast would the men react when she started swinging? Would she die before she could get her hand on a gun or lift the axe for a second swing?

Calming herself with an effort, she thought, *Not now. If I get desperate...*

Or was she hesitating out of cowardice?

No. She pictured Garrett's face, outwardly calm even

when his eyes were sharp with intensity. He wouldn't be far away. She *felt* him. As long as she was alive…

Right this minute, no one was threatening her. In fact, she had the impression that the men felt some wariness toward her. Maybe it stemmed from the usual male dislike of needing to depend on a woman for knowledge or skills they lacked. Did they see her as both their ace in the hole, as Cole put it, and a threat, too? Really, it was surprising when they listened, as they had when she hustled them by the mama bear.

Garrett was among the few men she'd known who bowed to her expertise without question, as he had when they climbed. Despite the background that left him unable to trust on an emotional level, his confidence in himself was solid enough that he could admire and take advantage of someone else's skills without feeling diminished himself.

Cole and Mason had let her take charge a couple of times, but she'd seen the anger simmering in their eyes.

Unfortunately, what confidence she'd been summoning dissipated in a slow trickle with the darkening sky. She decided reluctantly that she had scratched out as large a semi-level spot as was possible.

She leaned the ice axe casually against one of the tree trunks, within easy reach. "I think this works. There should be room for the three of us." And Cole wouldn't be able to drag her off into the darkness to rape her. Even he had to be smarter than that. Of course, this nice, wide spot would do fine if the two were into gang rape…

Mason hadn't given off that vibe, though. She felt sure that Cole was dominant; Mason had followed orders a number of times. Even so, would he just turn his back if—

Cadence cut herself off. Worry about it when the time comes. When she *had* to fight. Remember, Cole was wounded.

Mason looked more thoughtfully than she liked at the ice axe, then at her, but all he said was, "Let's spread that tarp and our pads. I'm hungry."

"Hungry? To hell with that!" Cole snapped. "You're not the one bleeding like a stuck pig!"

He pulled her own pack over to her, then hung over her like a vulture, thinking his meal was going to up and walk away while she dug in it. Mason stepped closer, too. Cadence reminded herself that they were bound to suspect she had a second handgun stowed away.

If only.

As Cole, grunting and complaining, pulled his shirt over his head and she used antiseptic wipes to cleanse his bloody upper arm, shoulder and chest, she tried really hard not to look closely, and especially not to breathe. She'd sweated all day, too, but he *stunk*. She did her best not to study his tattoos, crude compared to what she was used to seeing. Prison tattoos? she couldn't help wondering. Oh, and pretending his head wasn't *right there*, too, as he watched every move she made, was a challenge.

She had quite a pile of wipes by the time she had him clean enough to press a gauze pad to the hole that sullenly seeped more blood. "Can you hold this?" she asked.

He did without comment while she uncapped the antibiotic ointment and stacked a few gauze pads and readied the tape.

"There's no exit wound," she told him. "You'll need to have the bullet surgically removed as soon as possible." *If you're not dead.*

He grunted.

She went back to work, doing her best while blocking out the fact that she loathed this man. It was hard not to picture the frozen shock on the face of the dead climber as she worked to save Cole Whatever His Name Was.

Because the wound was high on the shoulder, it was hard to wrap. She ended up winding tape around his upper torso to help anchor the bandages.

"Do you have a clean shirt that will fit?" she asked finally. "This one—" she lifted it between thumb and forefinger "—is disgusting."

"No. I should dump most of what's in here." He lashed out with his booted foot and knocked over the pack she'd been hauling.

He was likely right, she realized. The surprise was that he and Mason hadn't already gone through their packs and discarded most clothing, if only to lighten their loads.

"Let me look," she said.

He removed her handgun from the outside pocket and pointed it at her. "Go for it."

More pretense. A big, square hand, fingernails filthy, wasn't holding a gun on her.

She worked fast, tossing most of the clothing aside. She could cut up that T-shirt to make a sling, if he'd be willing to wear one. Probably not, but she set it aside anyway. She finally found a Seattle Mariners sweatshirt that would certainly have been oversize on its owner and held it out. "Let's try this."

Mason made an irritated sound. "About time. We could have eaten first."

Cole lunged toward his friend, his good hand with the gun lifted as if he'd use it like a baton to beat Mason.

Mason managed to scramble back just in time. "What the—?"

Well, he said more than that. Cadence tried to unhear it.

And it wasn't as if she didn't hear foul language on a regular basis and even, in extremity, used it.

Cole answered in kind. Both of them seemed to puff up like those creatures in nature that made themselves look larger than they really were to repel predators—and these men were already massive.

She froze, doing her best to be invisible as they glared at each other.

Seemingly satisfied, Cole turned his attention to her. Not invisible.

"Why aren't you setting up the stove and cooking?"

Because that's what she'd been thinking. Let the two friends chat while she assumed her role as chef. Once she got her hands as clean as she could under the circumstances. Ugh. She didn't like the idea of his blood on her, but it had been unavoidable.

Her voice came out on a squeak. "I...was afraid the stove might get knocked over and set something on fire."

"Well, get on with it."

She hesitated. "I have Tylenol in that kit. Do you want some?"

His eyebrows drew together. "Of course I want some! Why didn't you give it to me before?"

"I'm sorry. It didn't occur to me."

He had more to say about that, of course. She tuned him out while she shook several pills into his hand and offered the water bottle.

Then she located the stove in his "borrowed" pack and set it up. When she pulled out packets of freeze-dried meals to see what they had, he snapped, "That stuff's crap." He eyed the packets in disgust. "It looks like dog food."

"That's what happens a lot of the time when you freeze-dry meals." These were a commercial brand undoubtedly bought at an outfitter's. "They usually taste fine. You just don't want to look at your food."

His eyes narrowed. "Bet you have something better."

Actually, she did, because she freeze-dried her own meals. Cadence used to love cooking. Lately, by the time she got home she was too tired to bother. Either that, or one or both roommates were already doing something in the cramped kitchen. She did occasionally, on a day off, make big batches of a couple of her favorites because they were superior to the commercial options.

Maybe better food would soften them a little, she thought ruefully. Her common sense muttered, *Right.* If Cole-the-creep's heart had a soft spot, she didn't want to find herself in it. She already hated the way he eyed her.

"I know I have a chicken marsala," she said, pulling her pack closer to her again.

"Is that some kind of foreign food?"

"Indian."

"Don't you have anything decent?"

She bit back what she'd like to say and dug to the bottom of her pack where the food often settled. "Beef stew."

"Now you're talking."

She took that for assent, asking if either had a full water bottle. If they hadn't used the purifying tablets, she thought boiling the water would kill any bacteria. She'd save what remained in her bottle for drinking.

She'd point out the tablets and suggest refilling bottles, except she hadn't heard the sound of a stream recently. There'd been one close to the trail early on, tumbling down the slope to join the Duckabush River. She had a feeling they wouldn't see another stream or river until they had descended from the pass tomorrow—if any of them ever made it so far.

She wondered if that was even Mason and Cole's real goal. What *did* they think would happen? They couldn't possibly be deluding themselves that holding her hostage would protect them while they strolled the many miles out to a road, where a friend would be waiting to pick them up in a car or truck that, of course, authorities would permit to drive away in peace. After all, a promise to release her once they were safely away was as good as gold, right?

An ache that felt more like a hollow seemed to expand. *Oh, baby.*

AFTER ERIC HANDED him a dish, Garrett nodded his thanks and ate mechanically. He had no idea what he was eating and didn't care.

Why hadn't those bastards contacted someone on Cadence's radio? Or were they waiting for morning, under the belief they had just cleverly vanished and could slumber unworried?

If the light had held up better, Garrett wouldn't have been able to prevent himself from attempting to follow. Probably that was just as well; with the terrain so difficult, he'd be bound to make some noise.

But waiting... It was killing him.

Aware Eric was watching him, he walled off any visible emotion.

"What if you try calling her?" the other man asked.

"She had it silent." He was sure he'd explained before. "We both did."

"What if they found it, and have been listening to everything said since?"

"They'd have had to do so almost immediately, and I can't see that happening." Explaining what felt obvious to him made him realize that even his jaw muscles were stiff. This took an effort. "They wouldn't have dared make a racket close to the trail. They knew how close behind I was."

Garrett had updated incident command—currently a deputy chief ranger—as soon as he discovered Cadence's ring and made assumptions he felt sure were accurate. In turn, he'd been put in the loop with the pair that had gone over the pass and were now looking for a place to bed down that put them close. Early morning, a helicopter was to return, drop another pair of law enforcement rangers on the slopes of Mount La Crosse, placing the prey—and Cadence—in the midst of a triangle. Where could they go? Especially since the helicopter had been charged to hover right overhead. That should pin the fugitives down and scare the you-know-what out of them. So far in their trek through the Olympic National Park, they hadn't felt seriously pressured. Why would they, with so many trails and so much wilderness to get lost in?

But taking this route, they'd made a mistake. He guessed they'd discovered quickly that their cell phones didn't work, and therefore they saw no way to negotiate until a park ranger offered herself as their hostage in place of the boy they'd taken originally.

Now it was a waiting game.

Garrett couldn't see himself sleeping, even if he and Eric took shifts. God. He felt as if fire ants were crawling all over him as it was, and at least for the moment, he had to make desultory, low-voiced conversation, help clean up after the meal he hadn't tasted and go through the motions of laying out pads and sleeping bags.

What if he hadn't screwed up so terribly with Cadence after that lunch when she confronted him about his feelings? Would anything have changed? If they'd taken a couple of days off to talk out emotions—he winced—and future plans, might she have been working a different shift when all this started? No matter what, she'd have been summoned to join the pursuit, but she might have taken Don Phillips's place advancing up the Duckabush. If that had been the case, Garrett sure as hell would have chosen Eric to keep moving with him while sending Cadence back with the poor kid.

Lying back on his sleeping bag, staring up at what stars he could see between dense evergreen growth, he pictured that. No, he wouldn't have been in a position to send Cadence anywhere, because this was *her* jurisdiction, not his. She and Eric would have discussed it, and she might well have won that battle and be lying next to him now.

Still safe, he thought.

And…he wouldn't have let her win, even if he had to tell the other man she was pregnant. She'd be mad as hell, but alive and *really* safe.

Instead, he closed his eyes, knowing he'd give anything to hear her voice, soft in the darkness. To be able to roll toward her, gather her into his arms, feel the trust that he'd thrown away.

Chapter Sixteen

Cole held her radio, his blistering stare finding her. "Why didn't you tell us you had this?"

"It doesn't work like a phone, you know." Cadence could not afford to lose her composure. If she cowered from them, they'd start terrorizing and hurting her. She knew it. "You can't call some friend."

She could tell he didn't like her answer, but bought it.

"Who can we call?"

"Olympic Park Dispatch, who'd put you through to whoever is coordinating the search for you—" *hunt* didn't seem like a wise choice of words "—and eventually, if necessary, a ranger or sheriff's deputy who is closest."

Garrett. Please, Garrett.

Cole looked as close to thoughtful as he was probably capable, bouncing the radio in his big, filthy hand.

Cadence had had to bed down compressed between the two men. Fear had all but electrified her. Cole had squeezed between her thighs, laughed when she stiffened and said, "Maybe tomorrow." If he'd gone for her breast, he'd have come up against the stiff bulletproof vest. She had to wonder if they had forgotten she wore it. She couldn't imagine they hadn't noticed it at all.

Cole, at least, snored, so she'd been able to tell when

he slept. Mason must have slept, but quietly. She'd never had a single chance to slip out from between the two of them and get her hands on one of their rifles or the oh-so-tempting ice axe.

The result was, sleep for her had been snatched in what felt like ten- or fifteen-minute increments. Naturally, she'd been awakened by a rough shake and ordered to make them something to eat. She hadn't even had that realization, *Oh, God, I'm a hostage.* No, the powerful need to throw up even what little she had in her stomach had driven her.

She'd gurgled something, crawled out of her sleeping bag and a few feet away so she could heave. Since she'd actually eaten her share of the stew, enough came up for whichever man had stepped aggressively toward her to retreat.

When she finished, she closed her eyes and let her head hang.

There was a moment of silence.

"What the hell?" Cole growled. "That's disgusting. You're not sick, are you?"

Oh, that was something for them to worry about: catching a stomach virus.

Mason, who tended to keep his mouth shut, said, "Hey, you're not…?"

No, no, no. Don't let that *idea enter their heads.*

"It's the ribs," she mumbled. "When I started to sit up… I don't know. I hurt and had to puke, too. It's like my body thinks I can expel whatever's wrong."

Mason never did finish his thought, thank goodness.

Cole, charming as ever, snapped, "Well, cover up that disgusting mess and get your butt over here to make breakfast."

Dear God. If she'd really been sick, she couldn't imagine how she would have complied. As usual, her stomach felt better, at least. The rest of her would feel fine once she rinsed her mouth out.

Neither remarked on her brushing her teeth before breakfast.

They weren't happy to learn their options were oatmeal with raisins, or oatmeal with dried apricot chips.

"It's quick, it's hot, it tastes good and it's filling," she informed them. "If you hate oatmeal, you can snack on granola and nuts instead."

Oatmeal it was.

She had just finished cleaning up when Cole started digging through her pack, tossing out the contents as he went. He'd gotten about halfway when it occurred to him to check the outer pockets, which was when he'd come up first with her phone, which he tossed, too, then with the radio.

She stacked the last few dishes together, then sank down cross-legged on the thin pad she had yet to roll and stow away.

Cole kept glaring at her. She raised her eyebrows.

"If I want to talk to someone, who should I ask for?"

"I'd suggest the man I was with when you grabbed me. I assume he's in immediate charge, and you know he isn't far away."

"What's his name?"

"Garrett Wycoff. He's a sheriff's deputy rather than a park ranger. A lot of the people looking for you are."

His lip curled. "Cops."

Gee, maybe because you committed multiple crimes?

"Park law enforcement are cops, too, you know." Not a good time to remind him that, even worse, they were *federal* law enforcement.

"Let's get moving," he said suddenly. "Pack everything up, in case we have to spend another night out here."

Mason looked at him with open incredulity, which Cadence shared.

She was careful to limit her response to nodding at the heap in front of her pack. "Are you done with all that?"

As if reminded, he stuck his arm in the pack and rooted around, coming up with a few hard objects: a pack of batteries for the flashlight, an extra fuel canister for the stove and her electronic reader, which was undoubtedly drained of battery power. In each case, he glanced, dropped them back in and then rose to his feet.

"Do it."

Their packs were scarcely disturbed from the night before, since she'd done the cooking using food she'd packed, and the stolen clothes they still carried didn't fit anyway. Mason did roll up Cadence's mat and hand it to her while she folded clothes and had to stuff it all back where it had come from. What almost might be consideration startled her.

She'd used quite a few meals by now, but they weren't space intensive, and Cole's arm had worked like a mixer in pancake batter. Now, with him standing above her, radiating impatience and the never entirely buried anger and hint of violence, she didn't dare take time to do a good job.

She stuffed, shoved her feet in her boots and tied them, then rose, too. And, oh, she ached, but that was nothing compared to the stab of pain in her torso. She pressed a hand to the exact spot. Why hadn't she thought to take some ibuprofen with the oatmeal? Only, was ibuprofen safe to take when she was pregnant? She probably should know, but either didn't or was too stressed to summon even common knowledge.

She glanced around, just as she always would when

packing up to move on, and saw that the ice axe still leaned exactly where she'd left it.

With two sets of eyes on her, she didn't just snatch it. Instead, she gestured. "We should take that. It's a useful tool and makes a good walking stick besides. Especially in rough conditions. That's why mountain climbers carry them."

Nope—mountain climbers rarely paused to envision killing someone with their ice axe. She congratulated herself for calling the tool "that," instead of by name. "Axe" had a whole different connotation.

Cole said impatiently, "Fine. Stick it back on my pack where it was."

He turned so she could do just that. Unfortunately, Mason continued to watch carefully.

Mason, she was beginning to think, was the brains of the pair, Cole the weapon he loosed when necessary. Cadence wondered if Cole realized his place. Clearly, he thought *he* was the alpha. Or was it possible they hadn't been long-term partners, and Mason was discovering that Cole was more than a little off?

"Ready?" Cole tipped his chin. "Up."

GARRETT WAS RELUCTANT to advance up the trail until he'd been assured Don Phillips and a couple of deputies from Jefferson County had started to the pass behind him and Eric. He thought it unlikely in the extreme that Cole and Mason would think they could safely rejoin the trail to climb to the pass…or to head back down the way they had come, thinking that would be a surprise to their pursuers.

That said…did they have any idea how tough it would be to scramble up a ridge so steep without a trail? And one that was thickly overgrown with everything from low-growing salal and Oregon grape to devil's club and huckle-berries? Such evergreens as grew here weren't the friendly kind that held out branches to be convenient handholds, ei-ther. In fact, their lowest branches tended to be high above human reach.

Or, hey, to scramble *down*? That, he suspected, would be even tougher. Sooner or later, someone's feet would go out from under them, and the fall could be long and painful.

Just sitting here rubbed at Garrett, and he decided to gamble that the men would head up, thinking the pass wasn't far above them. Difficult, though, to see how they thought they'd be able to negotiate a way out of here, but that had to be what they were thinking by this time. Ca-dence wouldn't be much use to them otherwise.

And, man, he hated thinking of her as a pawn.

Even though the crackle and voices would permit anyone nearby to pinpoint his and Eric's location, Garrett now mon-itored radio traffic. He needed to know who was where… and to be available if those murderous slugs decided it was time to talk their way out of the trap they'd gotten them-selves into after their poorly planned spree.

He kept an eye on his watch. They wouldn't have slept in, any more than he'd been able to. He had to assume they were on the move, and not far from him and Eric…or the twosome who had started down from La Crosse Pass half an hour or so ago.

The sun was rising higher than he'd expected, making him begin doubting himself by the time Dispatch connected to him, asked for confirmation of his call-in and informed him that Ranger Jones wanted to speak to him on behalf of Cole Souza.

Late yesterday, Garrett had learned both men's last names. They'd surely understood that fingerprints from their truck would open a book on both of them for law enforcement.

Souza had served a ten-year term in the Monroe Correctional Complex northeast of Seattle for second-degree murder. Mason Fitch was on record because of several traffic violations and an accident for which he'd been charged, but got off with a hand slap. Garrett wanted to think that knowing their criminal histories wouldn't make any difference in how Cadence responded to them. If Cole was the more volatile of the two, she'd have noticed by now. She had a gift for easing tempers, he'd noticed before, and relating to most people he and she had encountered.

"Standing by," he said into the radio.

"Garrett?"

Cadence's voice cracked. Or was the effect from being on the airways? He hoped so.

"It is," he said, going for calm. "Are you all right? Have you been hurt—"

He heard something muffled, then a man came on. "Cut the BS. We have things to talk over."

"I agree," Garrett said. "But I'm not prepared to discuss your situation until I hear Ranger Jones herself tell me that she hasn't been injured. This is nonnegotiable."

"You heard him," the voice snapped, and Cadence came back. "I'm injured, but not—" A man's voice burst out in the background. "Give me a second!" she snapped, her fiery response soothing Garrett's suppressed fear and fury. "I was *about* to say, I fell yesterday after we left the trail. You know how steep the ridge is. Neither Mason nor Cole has hurt me."

"All right," he said. "How badly—"

"I think a rib or two," she said hastily, but Cole was back. Or was it Mason?

"She was clumsy. Now can we talk?"

"We can."

Eric hovered close, his gaze on Garrett's face. Garrett didn't meet his eyes, afraid of how much he might give away.

"You in charge of where that helicopter goes?"

Garrett had been aware that it had been flying a slow pattern over the ridge this morning.

"I am the person you need to speak to," he agreed, which was far from the truth, but he'd seized the authority to negotiate, and he'd use any resources necessary to accomplish his goals: get Cadence safely back in his arms and nail these two bastards. "I'll have to clear any demands to use the helicopter with other people."

"Then you're not in charge."

"Neither the park service nor either county where you committed crimes owns a helicopter. We have arrangements to borrow one. As I said, I'm here to listen to what you want, and I'll get back to you once I have questions or answers."

Silence followed. Since these two were trapped like a calf in a chute, he didn't worry that they'd decide they didn't need him.

"We'll need a lift," the voice said. "Pilot only, unarmed. If I see a gun, I'll shoot him, and you can find a different one."

"Shooting a pilot will dig you deeper in a hole. You can't afford that."

"One body, two bodies…" He was undoubtedly shrugging.

"That would make three," he said flatly.

"Don't matter."

Oh, it mattered, as he would soon discover.

"You planning to fly far?" he asked.

"You think I'll tell you that?"

"The 'copter has been in the air quite a while this morning already. Unless you're thinking about a real short haul, it will need to refuel before it's any use to you."

"Do it."

Garrett nodded at Eric, who moved a distance away to open a communication on his own radio—assuming there was an effort this morning to prioritize their needs.

"What's the rest of the plan?" he asked.

"Like I'm going to tell you?" he sneered. "Not like you can't track us in the air anyway."

Garrett pictured a fighter jet screaming right above, keeping a *very* close eye on that helicopter and its occupants.

"Somebody will be able to," he agreed. No point in pretending.

Damn, even his experience as a negotiator wasn't helping him maintain the composure and dispassion he needed. Envisioning Cadence's face, her smile, helped in one way and not at all in another. "I meant that you'll have to tell me where you want the helicopter to set down to pick you up."

"Pass, but not right on the trail. Maybe we'll lay out stuff from the packs to make a circle."

"Noted. In exchange for the helicopter and the pilot's willingness to offer himself up as a hostage, we need you to show some good faith by releasing the woman."

The rude laugh was about what he'd expected, but he had to try.

"You're asking for a lot," he said mildly. "It's not unreasonable of us to expect you to give a little."

A snort. "Yeah, you can't tell me the pilot won't be a cop of some kind."

A US Navy airman, actually.

"If he goes into this unarmed…"

"How am I supposed to know he really is until I'm in the copilot seat with the barrel of my gun shoved against his temple? No, as long as we have this pretty lady, we have you by the short hairs. I don't think you have the balls to come in with bullets flying when she's in the middle of it."

Garrett ground his teeth together. That was putting it succinctly. He didn't know, though, how he could handle seeing her shoved into the helicopter, maybe looking for him over her shoulder, and then it lifting off. Would she become less necessary to them then, or would they still deem her their best safeguard for the few minutes after the helicopter set them down for another attempt at a getaway? And even then. From their point of view, why not haul her along? The kid would have worked as well, but they hadn't lost anything with the exchange.

The only difference, Garrett believed, was that she was an experienced law enforcement officer. She'd be calculating at all times, looking for an opportunity to take them off-balance.

He just hoped she wasn't too reckless when she thought she saw an opening. If she was killed—

The taste of bile rose in his throat.

"Let me talk to her again."

"He wants to say his bye-byes." Cole shoved the radio at her.

Cadence accepted the radio. If only she could think of a single thing she could tell him that would help him find them. She couldn't imagine she'd have any hope of doing anything but what they told her to when the terrifying moment came to walk into the open to the waiting helicopter.

She turned her head to see nothing distinctive. They had

scrabbled upward for what she estimated to be three hours already, but the going was so slow she had no idea how close they might be to mounting the ridge. One tree looked much like the next…except she could tell they'd entered a band of what was called montane forest, high enough in elevation that the trees grew slowly and any understory—the plant tangle that had tripped them up easily—diminished. She was able to spot some silver fir as well as the Douglas fir and western hemlock. None were huge even if they were old, given their precarious grip on the steep sidehill.

"Hey," he said, calm but…gentle. "You heard that?"

"Yes." They planned to use her until the bitter end. These were exactly the circumstances that led to a hostage being killed, as likely by friendly fire as by the bad guys. "Evan is okay?"

"Yep. The helicopter took him back to the campground, where he was reunited with his grandparents *and* his parents. He…had some things to pass on to you, but this probably isn't the time."

"No." A numbness seemed to be creeping over her. "Is the helicopter going to make it back today?"

"So far as I know."

"Okay." Why Cole in particular hadn't cut her off, she didn't know, but she wanted to get this out. "Some of what you said…you were right. It's not just for my sake I wish—"

Cole wrenched the radio from her hand. "That's it."

Garrett was trying to say something, but Cole shut him off. His narrowed eyes zeroed in on her face. "You and that guy. You got something going?"

"Don't be ridiculous," she said coolly. "We talked a bunch the past couple of days, that's all."

"Well, damn. This might've been even more fun if you did."

Mason intervened. "Let's move. We need to get in position while there's still plenty of daylight."

Cadence wondered what they would do if she crumpled and said, *I can't go any farther.*

Shoot her, the way Cole had suggested? Take turns using a fireman's carry to haul her carcass along whether she wanted to go or not?

Imagining her belly and rib cage crushed against one of those shoulders was all she needed to give her a second wind. There was pain…and then there was agony.

Chapter Seventeen

Nobody Garrett consulted with was surprised by the demands. What other options could there be? *Beam me up, Scotty?* From the minute the men had been pushed into turning onto a dead-end road, the possibilities diminished to near zero.

Unfortunately, they had a strong ace in their hands: Cadence.

Garrett might have lost it if anyone, including the chief ranger or county sheriff had so much as implied that she was any less than number one on their priority lists. If they'd been able to hold on to the boy, too, even Cadence would have put him first. Garrett tried to clutch onto that one positive: Evan was safe.

The pair that had been descending to meet him and Eric turned around. His reasonable assumption was that Cole and Mason would stop just before the tree line, when they lost their cover. That left only the mystery about where they'd pop out. Not expecting to hear from them any sooner, he and Eric hauled ass to reach that same tree line.

He briefly conferred with the others that he was now directing, but not a one of them knew this pass well. Alyssa Bailey, the triathlete, had hiked it, but had been wrapped up in the magnificent sweep of mountains, with no reason to study the immediate terrain for places flat enough for a helicopter to set down. A skilled pilot could load with just one skid on the ground if necessary, but that would be less than ideal for a lot of reasons.

What he was set on was taking the two down *before* they reached the helicopter. That would involve finding them, while remaining unseen. Maybe once they reached the ridgetop, Cadence would be able to offer a hint that would permit him to move into position.

Assuming he was allowed to speak to her again, he thought wryly.

And what could she possibly say? *I estimate we're three to four hundred yards west.* Sure. And west of the trail near the pass would involve more climbing, as Mount La Crosse reared directly west, the trail cutting across the slope.

This was magnificent country, he was reminded when the view opened ahead of them. Mountains everywhere, snow clinging in shadowed hollows, the rock gray and intimidating. Wildflowers and the small, windswept alpine fir in clusters. He'd forgotten there was a small lake and few puddles in the basin east of the pass. Better ground for a helicopter to land over there. Would Cadence suggest it to them? Would they listen to anything she did suggest?

The distance from the pass to the lake was too open for them to be willing to trot to it—unless they'd crossed the trail behind Garrett and Eric to edge that direction.

Now, that *was* the kind of thing she might have suggested.

The radio remained silent. He and Eric would have made better time, Garrett reminded himself.

Two rangers sat in plain sight right at the pass, but they stood and trotted toward Garrett and Eric when they appeared.

He'd not met them before. They were the two men who had already been in the so-called Enchanted Valley area tucked beneath Mount Anderson. One had white-blond hair, wasn't over five foot eight or nine, and was almost slender. Garrett had a feeling the unprepossessing appearance was deceptive, however. The guy could well be a distance runner, like Alyssa Bailey. The other was closer to Garrett's height, solidly built, face at least two days from a shave, eyes steady.

They moved to a clump of silver fir and a few small western hemlocks to be out of sight, then shook hands all around. Garrett answered questions, filling them in on what they hadn't heard and telling them his best guesses.

"I know Cadence," said the thin one, who'd introduced himself as Nathan Ryback. "We did some cross-country skiing not long after she was hired."

"I've met her, too," Davis Bourke agreed.

Garrett felt a surge that was painfully close to jealousy. He'd felt an instant rapport with Bourke, a sense that they'd understand each other...and that they had enough in common physically, Cadence might be drawn to him.

He shook off the personal pang that had no place here, and said, "I'd like to know about your backgrounds. For example, have either of you had sniper training?"

Bourke bent his head in acknowledgment. "I have. I was army for ten years. Decided to go into law enforcement when I got out, thought I'd like a lot of open space and ended up at the Grand Canyon."

"I hear it's busier than Times Square in New York City."

"Yeah, not quite what I had in mind."

"Have you kept up at the range?"

"Not usually at the distances I once could do, but enough."

"Good. I don't know how you feel about it, but—"

Bourke's face hardened. "I feel fine. After they gunned down a sheriff's deputy and then some poor sucker who was here in the mountains for fun? And then there's Cadence." He was clearly done.

Garrett nodded acknowledgment. With Eric, that made two decent sharpshooters. That was pure luck, given how few of them were here.

"All right. I'm hoping we can get close, but until we know where they're going to emerge and expect the helicopter to land, we can't make any solid plans. Oh, we should have three more people with us shortly. Eric's partner, Don Phillips, and two Mason County deputies, if I remember right."

Eric nodded.

"You've talked to Cadence." That was Ryback.

"I have. As I told you, she apparently took a fall hard enough that she thinks she has broken ribs. It's…causing some nausea, too." He assumed she'd hidden the real reason for her on-again, off-again nausea from Cole and Mason, as he would now. "Far as I know, she's still on her feet, and we know what tough conditions they're in. She's quick thinking, and if she's strong enough to make it up here, we shouldn't count her out as help."

There were nods all around.

He hated waiting.

WHEN THEY REACHED the trail, Mason and Cole had both settled their rifles in firing position, one looking downhill, the other up. Cadence tried to remember who was supposed to be where and couldn't put the pieces together. She'd lost any reliable sense of how much time had passed. She just thought intensely, *Whoever was supposed to be on their way up...don't. Not now.*

Nobody appeared. She and the two men actually half jogged up a brief stretch of the trail before reluctantly—on her part—returning to the cover of the trees and the steep rock and soil she kept skidding on. Any patience either man had felt for her had eroded. She didn't dare hold them up. It was surprising enough that they'd taken her advice to risk showing themselves by crossing and climbing what quickly felt like even more difficult terrain to the east side of the trail. Still, it was her job to make sure they saw a realistic rendezvous point atop the pass once they reached it. She convinced herself that Garrett would prefer that, too. He'd need someplace that he could conceivably surround them for an assault.

When her stomach turned over this time, she couldn't blame pregnancy. No, it was the picture of her in the middle of an assault team. There had to be a way she could take herself out of the picture. There had to be. Because otherwise...

No. She paused long enough to wipe sweat off her brow and breathe deeply. Sacrificing herself wasn't on the agenda, and she felt sure Garrett would never consider that as a plan or even a possibility. He'd throw himself over her first. What did matter was stopping Mason and Cole before they got in that helicopter and pressed a gun barrel to another hapless hostage's head, this one who'd volunteered himself.

Like she hadn't?

That hadn't been her intention. Only freeing Evan. As awful as this was, better her than an eleven-year-old boy. And...there was the vest. If she could avoid literally being held upright as a shield, if she could drop flat...

She kept reverting to what she could do if this or that happened. Somehow, she also paid attention to her next handhold, if there was one, to making sure each step was solid before committing to it.

"WHERE'S THE GODDAMN HELICOPTER?"

Garrett crouched behind a rock and the feathery branch of a stunted fir, hoping his tan cargo pants and long-sleeve, faded green shirt were adequate camouflage.

He pressed his thumb to reply. "I'm told it's not far out. I don't hear it, either."

"I want it to land as close to the tree line as possible. I see some puddles out there. I expect it to be south of those."

"I'll let them know. I can't guarantee a particular landing zone. I'm not a pilot."

"You can see a flat place as well as anyone else. No excuses."

"I need to talk to Ranger Jones," he said in a hard voice. "This deal is entirely dependent on her well-being."

After a momentary silence, he heard her hesitant, "Garrett?"

"That's me."

"I don't think my thigh muscles will ever recover."

He chuckled. That had been one hell of a steep climb. "At least there weren't any more trees down across the trail the last ways."

"No? Well, the ones up here are built to bend before wind and snow. Except—"

"What are you telling him?" a man asked roughly in the background.

"I'm not telling him anything!" she snapped. "We're just talking. I like to hear a friendly voice."

"Do what you're told and you'll hear one again."

"Sure." Her sadness and disbelief leaked through.

Garrett shared that fear. "You still hurting?"

"Of course I am." Now she was more subdued. Cole's hand probably hovered inches away, ready to snatch the radio. "I'm trying not to, um—"

"That's enough!" one of the men growled, and the connection was severed.

Kneeling beside him, Eric raised his eyebrows. "Get anything from that?"

Garrett bent his head for a moment. *Get a grip.* Then he said roughly, "Yeah. Couple of things." He surveyed the land in their vicinity. Whether it had been their idea or Cadence's, the pair must have done as Garrett had guessed they might: they'd crossed the trail at some point to place them near the shallow basin here. And…yeah. There it was.

He pointed toward one of the thicker clusters of the stunted evergreens that were about all that survived at this elevation, and as exposed to the elements as they were. "Top of the tree's snapped off."

Eric's gaze followed his. "How did you get that?"

"She commented on how the trees are flexible enough to bow before any strong winds. And then she said, 'Except…' That's the only tree I see with the top broken off."

"Well, damn." Eric pondered. "Do we try to move on them?"

They were close; so close, Garrett cautioned the other man not to make sudden movements that would draw the eye. "It's too risky. They're watching for us. We'd be crossing open ground. If we can coordinate with Don it would be one thing, but right now I think it's best if we stay off the radio except for touching base with the helicopter pilot and Souza and Fitch."

Eric sighed. "What if the damn thing lands *between* us and them, and blocks us?"

"We suggest a different place to set down." Should he say anything about Cadence's last suggestion, as abortive as it had been? He grunted. He had to prepare his partner as well as he could. "There at the end," he said. "I think she was letting us know that she'll use her nausea, real or pretend, to delay or drop to the ground when she thinks the moment is right."

"How's that going to protect her? Or is it her idea of a signal?"

He stretched his neck to one side until it cracked, then to the other side. "Don't know. If they think she's just diving for cover, they might shoot her then and there. They might hesitate if she's puking. Keeping her as a hostage is essential to their plan to somehow disappear when their ride ends."

Eric studied him quizzically. "You think that's what she was talking about when she said she's trying not to do something?"

"I do think. She wasn't finished with what she was trying to say."

They lapsed into silence. The sun continued moving across the sky, the delay excruciating. Garrett began to feel chilled. Would they let Cadence add another layer? He didn't want her to be cold.

Had someone higher up blocked the use of a helicopter to transport a pair of killers, given that their expressed intention had been to hold a gun on the pilot? Were no pilots willing? But Garrett didn't believe it, given that machine and pilots both were US military.

Usually a patient man, Garrett stayed rigid, his skin prickling. He hated not being in complete control. Maintaining readiness for an operation that could happen anytime—ten minutes or two hours—always felt this way. Life and death decisions weren't new to him...but they'd never before involved the woman he loved.

By this time, using the word didn't even surprise him.

A QUIVER RAN over Cadence when she first heard the helicopter. It was definitely approaching.

"That's it!" Cole snapped. "Everyone on their feet and ready."

"What?" Mason said. "We're just going to run out there and wave, 'Here we are! Shoot us?'"

This argument hadn't changed, and they were still at it. Personally, she gave thumbs-up to Mason's side. Partly because authorities in the form of park law enforcement and deputies weren't going to let two men who'd already killed stroll out and hop into the helicopter just because they were ushering her along with them. They'd try not to shoot her, but that was no guarantee. She even understood. Garrett might be fighting on her side, but likely someone with park law enforcement was in charge by this time.

She had the fleeting thought, *If he let them be.*

Cole glowered. "I should have thrown something out to tell that pilot where to land, like I said."

"And that wouldn't have given away where we are?" Mason said in disbelief.

Please, Garrett, be nearby.

Here the 'copter came, the rotors whipping overhead so that the trees shook as if in a storm, the noise almost deafening. It passed almost overhead, but not quite; head back, she didn't see the pilot looking down, as she'd hoped she might.

At least one thing was on her side: her stomach was plenty ready to play its part. In fact, she'd been at least queasy for most of the day, more than usual. Because of stress? Or thanks to the sharp pain in her side? Either, or both?

Usually as soon as she was done puking, she could eat. This morning, she hadn't wanted to, but made herself. And during their brief stop to eat midday, she'd forced more down.

The helicopter settled slowly down on a piece of rocky ground closer than she had wanted, farther away than Cole and Mason had in mind.

"Get on the radio!" Cole screamed. "That's not good enough!" He added invectives that had Mason flushed and angry, too. Mason tried to connect with the radio, but static and voices didn't let him. He finally threw it down and lifted a big, booted foot with the clear intention of stomping on it.

Because that would do so much good.

Cole swung a fist at him, knocking him back. Cadence cowered from the outburst of violence, using what was surely a natural reaction to also open a few feet of separation.

Her pack? Leave it on? Take it off so she could move faster?

Wear it, she decided, as she had already done earlier. Along with her vest, it would give her some protection from gunfire.

A door in the helicopter opened and she saw a man in a helmet wearing headphones lean over to look at them. Apparently he *had* spotted them as he settled down. He waved his hand.

"The pilot," she said. "He's…he's signaling for us."

Mason and Cole snarled at each other again, then turned to look. The distance wasn't great. Maybe thirty yards?

Where was Garrett?

Had he understood her hint? Did he have his eye on them right now?

She wanted, quite fiercely, to believe he did.

She knew what she had to do, although this would surely go down in the annals of law enforcement as the most embarrassing way to self-protect ever.

Ruthless hands grabbed at her, pulled her roughly to place her to one side. She would have guessed that direction was their greatest vulnerability, too—unless the pilot was armed and started shooting. It was Mason who had her upper arm in a tight grip.

"Let's move." Cole was still giving the orders, although she intercepted a dirty look from his partner.

He held his rifle in firing position. Mason's remained slung over his shoulder, but he had his pistol in his free hand. Just before they stepped out of cover, he pushed the barrel against her temple.

She hadn't expected that, and it scared her more than anything else about the situation. She tried to tell herself to ignore the gun. He wouldn't keep pressing it to her head, would he? Cadence fixed her gaze on a slanted boulder ten or fifteen feet away. If she could throw herself behind it…

As if reading her mind, Mason's fingers dug hard into her flesh. "Don't screw this up," he murmured in her ear.

"I'm sick to my stomach," she whispered. "Can we wait? I think I need to—"

Not hearing her, Cole had stepped into the open, starting to move and rotating his rifle from side to side as he watched for any movement. Mason kept pace, Cadence stumbling. She gasped for breath, her heart racing. God, don't let *him* stumble, or his gun could go off.

They were close to the long, low ridge the slab of rock made.

She swallowed. "I *have* to—" So much for real heroism.

He glanced at her in some alarm. "Don't even think about it."

She pressed a hand to her belly beneath her rib cage, pushed as hard as she could bear and vomited.

"What the—?" Mason's hand jerked, the barrel lifting.

Cadence managed to turn her head far enough to send a stream of bile at him. He started swearing savagely even as she let herself fall as if to her knees. For a moment she hung from his hand, but in her peripheral vision, she saw movement, heard shouts.

"Drop your weapons! *Now!*"

Mason tried to lift her, but even for someone as powerfully built as him, deadweight was hard to control with one hand. The instant she felt the pain in her knees as they hit hard ground, she wrenched to free her arm. She had to roll.

Cole began shooting, spraying bullets far and wide. There'd be answering gunfire any second.

Chapter Eighteen

Despite their inability to communicate, Garrett saw out of the corner of his eye that Don Phillips and two other men had appeared to the far side of the fugitives. Too exposed, he knew, but like him they were all thinking about Cadence and her vulnerability.

Everything was happening too fast. He saw her seemingly trip and start to fall, and the instant of revulsion that distracted the man holding her. He kept his grip even as she started to go down, but at the first shouted order looked up.

Cadence hit the ground, flung herself full length and tried to roll. Not happening with that damn pack sticking out of her back, but she kept scrambling.

The SOB with the rifle hadn't taken his finger off the trigger, firing a fusillade covering nearly a hundred-and-eighty-degree arc. Bullets pinged off the helicopter, the door of which had closed. Garrett saw somebody go down—one of the men with Phillips. He himself had yet to fire, but now he did, close enough to have decided to rely on his handgun. Lifting the Glock with both hands, he didn't allow himself any distraction. Giving himself over to tunnel vision, he aimed for the thigh of the man shooting the rifle. Pulled the trigger. Once, twice. Again as his knees buckled, this time aiming for the upper arm or shoulder.

The rifle fell even as the man did. The others were running forward, bullets flying. Dangerous when the assault teams were on nearly opposite sides of the people they were trying to bring down. His own arm stung, but he kept closing in.

The second guy leaped toward Cadence, but Garrett thought it was Bourke who fired a warning shot right in front of his boots. The man lurched back, let his own gun fall to the ground and raised his hands.

Please, God, don't let her have taken a bullet.

Someone was cuffing the man who had now fallen to his knees, while Eric and Don Phillips stood over the man Garrett had shot. A wound in Phillips's thigh soaked his pants with blood. The one Garrett didn't recognize wasn't moving at all.

Garrett ran for Cadence, found her at the edge of a rock slab that protruded a few feet above the rest of the ground, the face she turned to him shocked, too pale, scratched and dirty. Her finely cut cheekbones were more prominent than they should be. She whimpered, scaring the crap out of him, and dry heaved a couple of times.

He all but fell next to her. "Are you hurt? Tell me you're not hurt."

"I'm...not hurt," she whispered. "Just..." She waved a hand.

He let a prayerful word escape and sank to his butt beside her. "I didn't know I could be that scared."

"Me, either. Ugh."

Garrett laughed. He'd have sworn he'd forgotten how, but damned if he didn't do it. Her expression was indignant, until he said, "Morning sickness as a tactical move. Never seen it employed before."

Her lips twitched. "I'm an original."

"Yeah." He swallowed and helped her slip out of the pack and push herself to her hands and knees. Then he decided he didn't care what anyone thought about them and gathered her into his arms. Thankful. So thankful.

"Do they all know?" she asked.

"Know what?"

"That I'm pregnant?"

"Oh. No. I let them think the nausea is because of your ribs."

She bit her already cracking lower lip, then tried to peer past him. "Are…are they dead?" she asked.

He must be blocking her sightline to the others. Garrett turned his head. "Not sure about the one. No, he's moving. I shot him several times myself. The guy who was dragging you along looks okay. He's got his hands in the air."

"Mason." She said the name so quietly he had to tilt his head to hear her. "He… I don't think he wanted to hurt me."

"Yeah? Didn't look that way to me."

"He's the more stable of the two. I suspect Cole is the one who did the shooting and probably killed the two men. Mason was…pretty frustrated with him."

"Shouldn't have gotten in the truck in the first place then, should he?" He knew how hard his voice was. "Given their planned activities."

"No." She tried for a smile that twisted. "I'm not nominating him for citizen of the year. Just…saying I don't think he's the killer."

"Okay." It was taking some time, but holding her allowed his heart to reset so it wouldn't pound through his chest wall, and his muscles to begin to relax after some belated twitches. "You know he'll be charged anyway."

Her head bobbed, bumping his scratchy chin. God, he wanted to kiss her, but—

He jerked when a voice spoke from right above him.

"Ranger Jones? You okay?"

This smile was weak but present. "More or less. Just taking a minute to get myself together."

It was Eric looking down at them. "Understandable."

Garrett pulled himself together. "Cadence says the one who is down is Cole Souza, the other Mason Fitch. Souza in bad shape?"

"Not good. The Clallam County deputy is badly injured, too. I don't like having them share a ride, but we don't have a lot of choice but to load him and Souza both onto this helicopter. Your…injuries don't look life-threatening, Cadence. If I'm wrong—"

"I can wait. I do think I have broken ribs, but I've hiked halfway up a mountain since I injured myself, and nothing has punctured my lungs yet."

That was upbeat. Garrett wanted to see her given priority, but she was right; her injuries weren't urgent. And that would give them some time to talk.

"Fitch will have to wait," Eric added. "We've got some other people hurt, too."

Cadence was looking at him. "You're bleeding," she said suddenly.

Both he and Eric glanced down at themselves. Garrett saw that the sleeve of his shirt was blood soaked and… Yeah, he found the tear, remembering the sting he'd felt.

"Nothing serious," he said.

"You've been shot in *both* arms now!" she exclaimed. "Don't tell me that isn't serious!"

Eric looked mildly surprised at her vehemence, but did glance at Garrett as if reminding himself that, yeah, his right upper arm was thickly bandaged.

Reluctantly Garrett decided he'd better check out the

wounded man and oversee the scene. He gently set Cadence aside, but she made motions as if she intended to stand, too.

He opened his mouth to tell her to stay put, but had the brains to understand that this was one of those moments that could make or break their relationship. So instead, he held out a hand and applied enough pull to get her back on her feet.

They left her pack where it was and picked their way toward the cluster of men around the one who was being edged onto a backboard.

At first sight, he'd have said their small force had multiplied, but that wasn't true. He counted: him and Eric, Don Phillips and the two he'd brought with him, and Bourke and Ryback. Then there was the guy in a flight suit who seemed to be overseeing the arrangements to load the deputy ahead of Souza. Garrett did wonder whether he'd come unarmed or not. Not, was his best guess.

Mason, on his knees, didn't raise his head. His hands were cuffed behind him. He was as filthy as the rest of them, visible skin scratched, but Garrett didn't see any blood.

Cadence took a step away from Garrett and laid a hand on the guy's shoulder. She said quietly, "You could have shot me."

Mason grimaced, still not looking up. "Lousy plan," he mumbled. "I don't do shit like that."

"Thank you," she said. "I'll speak for you to investigators."

The guy didn't say anything else, and Cadence walked to the helicopter to say a few words to the seriously injured man and to the pilot.

Then she looked around for her pack and called, "Anybody who is bleeding, come see me." She raised her eye-brows at Garrett. "Starting with you."

"I'll get the pack."

She opened her mouth, he quirked an eyebrow himself, and she shrugged acquiescence. He brought the pack to her.

The important stuff he had to say would have to wait.

A SECOND HELICOPTER carried everyone who was injured to the community hospital in Port Angeles on the north shore of the Olympic peninsula. Cadence felt a little guilty, looking out the window at the scene receding as they rose from the ground. The few people who were completely uninjured would be hiking out. She was intensely glad Garrett wasn't among them. Right this minute, she needed to be within touching distance of him, even though she was still confused about how to answer him.

The racket was too great to allow for conversation, but he sat right beside her, their shoulders pressed together. She couldn't care less if his blood was soaking into her uniform shirt. That shirt was destined for the trash, anyway.

She felt very strange. So much had happened. Examining her tangle of emotions, she realized she hadn't really believed she would survive. Garrett's determination and sheer competence couldn't have saved her if Mason had pulled that trigger...or if any of the other bullets flying around had struck her. Fear left her shaky, but a sense of weightlessness, as if she wasn't belted into a seat at all, was way more than relief. Hope was buoying her, she finally decided.

No one else seemed to be paying much attention to her, so she risked laying her hand on her abdomen. *We made it, baby. I'm so sorry I took any chances with you.*

When she glanced at Garrett, it was to see his gaze had followed her hand. When he lifted that gaze to meet hers, his expression was raw and she knew he had read her mind. Or maybe he'd been thinking the same thing anyway.

The next second, determination hardened his face. "You know what I want to say."

"Not the time."

He turned his head, grimaced and said, "Soon."

Would she be able to resist him? Should she?

She gazed out the window, then closed her eyes, tipped her head to touch his shoulder briefly, smiled and didn't meet his eyes until medical personnel met them at the hospital and steered them separate directions. Looking perturbed, his gaze didn't leave her until a curtain closed her into a cubicle.

A young woman doctor arrived almost immediately and examined her. "We need X-rays, of course."

Cadence lowered her voice to be sure she couldn't be heard on the other side of the curtain. "I'm pregnant."

"Ah. You're certain."

"I've done a couple of home tests. And I have morning sickness."

The doctor decided she needed to pee in a cup. The results of the urine test didn't take long.

The doctor smiled. "You're definitely pregnant. I assume you're happy about it?"

"Very."

"Do you have a partner who will be able to help?"

Probably not her business, but Cadence nodded.

With extra precautions being taken, she had the X-ray, which revealed two cracked ribs. Actually, the doctor's words were, *Only* cracked.

Thank you. Cadence rolled her eyes behind the woman's back.

In the end, she was wrapped a few inches below her

breasts in a mummy-like fashion, and prescribed a pain-killer the doctor assured her was safe. The doctor encouraged her to see an obstetrician soon, start on prenatal vitamins and consider not throwing herself off cliffs for the next seven months or so.

After filling the prescription, Cadence decided she needed to wait for Garrett. An aide carried her pack to the waiting room for her, where she sat. The next step—transportation—didn't seem very important right now, with so much going through her head. One certainty rose to the top: she had to resign from her job—or be transferred to a non–law enforcement capacity, if that was available.

From past experience, she doubted it was. If not…could she find another job locally? Or should she go home to Idaho?

But…what about Garrett?

Other people came and went, but sitting alone in her corner she knew the moment he came out of the back. His presence was that dominating. Even though his injuries were worse than hers, nobody carried his pack. He walked straight to her, those blue eyes never leaving her face. Truthfully, he looked as bad as she suspected she did: dirty, tired and moving carefully. His stubble was turning into a beard. He carried a paper bag with the pharmacy logo on it that matched hers.

"Hey," he said, stopping in front of her. "All patched up?"

She wrinkled her nose. "Literally." When she mentioned her mummy comparison, he chuckled.

"You and me both. Cracked sternum." He gingerly sat in the chair beside her.

"Two ribs."

"And your bullet wounds?"

"Wrapped anew. I don't think they did any better job

than you did. I have prescriptions for antibiotics and pain-killers."

"I already got mine. Um…maybe we can share a taxi home?"

"I called my grandfather. He's on the way to pick us up."

Us.

Cadence shifted uneasily. "Does he even know I exist?"

"Of course he does." His mouth twisted ruefully. "He's been giving me hell for not fighting for you."

She blinked at that. "You're serious?" And, "Is he okay to drive this far?"

"Yeah. He's doing great." Something shifted in his expression. "Let's go wait outside. I think there are benches."

After a moment, she nodded. Even with the advent of evening, the air was warm. She inhaled it and let Garrett steer her to the farthest bench from the entrance. Nobody would notice them here.

"You asked if I'm serious," he said after a moment. "Damn straight I am."

Cadence took a deep breath. "Just because you feel responsible—"

"I *am* responsible. But that's not the point."

"Of course it is."

He shook his head, sadness momentarily showing. "No, Cadence. I didn't want to admit it, but I'm in love with you. I want to marry you. I swear."

She straightened, winced but squared her shoulders. "When did you decide you were in love with me? When you thought I might die? That's sort of classic, isn't it? Pretty sure emotion born out of fear isn't lasting."

"No." He took her hand this time. "I ignored what I was feeling until you issued your ultimatum and I panicked."

"So I saw," she said tartly.

"When you drove away, I felt like I'd just been in a head-on crash. Dazed, disbelieving. Unsteady on my feet. I'd have been calling and knocking on your door any day. I just…had to come to terms with feeling something for you that I'd sworn I'd never let myself feel."

"I do understand," she said softly. "It's just…"

"Just what?"

"I couldn't bear it if you started to pull away." She had an awful lump in her throat. "If I could tell you were sorry for making a commitment like this."

"I will never be sorry." There was steel in his voice she'd heard when he was on the job, but never with her. "I knew you were different from the beginning. I was a coward, that's all. I want you to marry me. I *need* you to marry me. The idea of having a family—"

Had his voice thickened?

"I…want that, too," she admitted. "But I'm still scared. I can't decide if it would be worth having everything and then losing it, or starting off strong and on my own in the first place."

"You will never be on your own." He swallowed. "I love you, Cadence. I want to be a father. Please, will you marry me?"

She made herself just breathe for a minute, then said, "Maybe?"

"Maybe?"

"We don't have to decide today."

"And when do you decide?"

"Well, before the baby is born?"

He gusted out a breath. "You want to waddle down the aisle?"

Suddenly, she was smiling. "I won't wait that long. It's just…you should have time to be sure."

That's when his head tipped and his gaze sharpened, if such a thing was possible. "But you? You don't need time to be sure?"

"I've been in love with you for months," she admitted. "I let myself hope for longer than I should have."

He unexpectedly grinned, looking rakish. "I'll tell you what. Give me overnight, and we'll have this talk again."

"Overnight?"

"Sounds like plenty long to me." The smile had died, and he had the intent look on his face that she recognized. "Can I kiss you?"

Her eyes burned, but she reached for him even as she nodded.

The feel of him, the taste, was so familiar, and she knew she hadn't imagined the tenderness she'd always felt from him. Or the passion. His jaw was scratchy, but she didn't care as he claimed her mouth. She *wanted* him. His hand slipped around her nape, kneading, kneading, and she wanted to crawl onto his lap, but they *were* in public. And both injured.

He broke off the kiss to murmur against her lips, "By the way. I told Granddad we'd stop at your place and pick up some clean clothes and whatever else you need, and then you'd come home with us."

Her mouth opened and closed a few times, guppy-like, before she laughed. "You might try *asking.*"

"Yeah, the asking wasn't going so well, but I figured you wouldn't hurt my grandfather's feelings by refusing. I think that's his truck I hear."

Part of her wanted to hold out, to demonstrate her stubbornness and independence, but really, she couldn't think of anything she'd like better than going home with Garrett. And, hey, it wasn't as if her current digs were all that great.

Plus…by including his grandfather—his only family—
he was showing that he was all in. How could she resist that?

So she said, "Well, if you have better water pressure
than mine."

With a hand on his chest, she felt the rumble of his laugh
as much as heard it. "I'm sure we do."

She'd complained before about the pathetic drizzle that
she called a shower.

"Do you have a bathtub?" she thought to ask.

"Umm-hmm. Claw-footed. Deep enough to swim in. If
we could get Granddad out of the house, we could share it."

The rusty creak of a door slamming came to her ears.

"You win."

The gleam in his eyes joined with his grin. "What do
I win?"

And she laughed. "You'll have to wait and see." Her
gaze went past him to the tall, only slightly stooped, white-
haired man who approached. Somehow he'd spotted them
with no trouble. She'd have known he was related to Garrett if she'd happened on him at the grocery store anytime
these past few months.

He raised a white eyebrow at her, and she stood, smiling, to meet him.

It only got better when Garrett rose, pulled her close
and said, "Granddad, meet your soon to be granddaugh-
ter, Cadence Jones."

Really? She was going to surrender this easily? Of course
she was, she admitted. How could she say no when the man
she loved offered her everything she'd ever wanted?

And all she had to do was remember the desperation
she'd seen in his eyes several times the past few days to
know he wanted it all, too.

* * * * *